Fixed Ideas

FIXED IDEAS

Translated by Duncan J. Lewis

nordisk books

Published by Nordisk Books, 2021

www.nordiskbooks.com

© Eline Lund Fjæren

First published by Forlaget Oktober AS, 2018

Published in agreement with Oslo Literary Agency

This English translation copyright © Duncan J. Lewis, 2021

This translation has been published with the financial support of NORLA

Cover design © Nordisk Books

Printed and bound in Great Britain by Clays Ltd, Elcograf S.p.A.

A CIP catalogue record for this book is available from the British Library

ISBN 9781838074234

eBook ISBN 9781838074241

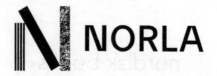

He wanted to fuck her loudly on a hard bed
with rain beating on the windows.

– Don DeLillo, Mao II

Part One

He helps her to loosen the clasp on her bra. Sweat from her back clings to his index finger. He considers wiping it on the pillow case. But he probably knows what she will think if he does this. What makes him hesitate is a sudden creasing of her brow that is visible when she sees him staring at his own finger and so catches him thinking something she does not wish him to be thinking, especially not about her body. The elasticated sheet is blue, with a couple of shiny patches at the left corner of the bottom end. She waits for him to touch her breasts. She sits on the bed and poses with the help of some gestures she has picked up from the movies and TV shows, he thinks, maybe pornography. There is something pornographic about the way she is acting; with her tits towards him, she smiles, apparently effortlessly and brightly. He kneels down next to her, crouching by the side of the bed. When she asks what he wants to do with her, his legs tremble a little perhaps, but not so much that it becomes a problem; they remain steady on the ground. He supports his left elbow on his knee. If anyone were watching them from above, they would possibly think they were witnessing a marriage proposal. His head is at the same height as her pelvis, he stares straight at her genitals, feels it is far less of a problem to stare in that direction than, for example, into her eyes. When he feels that he has kept this gaze for too long, he lowers his head and looks down at the floor. He thinks about how the muscles envelop the skeleton, how they bind and tighten. She lifts a foot and stretches her toes towards his shoulder, she is unsure of how she should act; an awareness of her own nakedness becomes at the same time an awareness in him. This position means that he can see deeper inside her. She squeezes her toes around his shoulders. A ring of muscle in her leg becomes visible as she pulls him towards her.

She doesn't want to go down on him before she's had something to drink, she says. The rain hammers against the windows. It's too stuffy in here, he thinks, he hasn't got round to buying a summer duvet. They are sweating, she needs some water. He goes out to the kitchen.

The kitchen work surface was dappled with light, it was summer and he was not in love with her, that's not what this is about. They had been at a party for the newspaper where they both work, the boss's enormous garden was decorated beyond all reason, with lanterns and various drapes hanging from the trees, glass bowls of punch, like something from a film. She tried to pull him into the bathroom with her, she's that type, without quite knowing what it is he means, but it surprised him; with her innocent appearance, the round face, big, blue eyes. She's young, but her body is that of an adult, almost motherly, that is how he would describe her, even if the thought repels him. She is slim, but with round hips and breasts. She came over to him at the party and kissed him in front of their colleagues, that's clearly how she does it, or young women do, they "take charge," know what they want, is it old fashioned of him to think about it like that, is it not the case? But doing it in the toilets, he drew the line there. He invited her home, suggested that they could take a taxi, he would pay, he earns more than her, something he of course did

13

not point out other than by offering to pay. She hesitated at the suggestion, as if she really just needed a quick fuck and that it had to be in the toilets, that it was not intimacy she was looking for, something made her initiative seem mainly like a sudden impulse, almost a need and one which didn't even seem to have anything to do with him, other than the fact that he was the youngest of her male colleagues and therefore the most compatible. He was too drunk to think it through any further.

When she saw his bedroom, she started to laugh, and he to regret it, at least for a moment. She mocked him about his bed, a single bed, he was thirty-six years old and slept in a single bed? It was humiliating, unnatural, she said, childlike. He is fourteen years older than her, she called him childlike. They were so drunk, making out for a long time without taking their clothes off, she fell out of the bed, he could see that she was embarrassed, it was so visible that she was drunk, you were supposed to hide it, just drink enough to make it possible to hold a conversation without the usual film of restraint and awkwardness, she had overdone it, had to recover herself again. Your bed, she said, I'm just going to fall out. He apologised, kissed her, guided his hand in under her shirt, caressed her breasts.

She asks him to inspect her. He knows that she has been sick, she has written about it in the paper. She is unable to check her own body, wants him to do it. To be a father for her, maybe, but to fuck her hard, to control her. She goes down on him first, for a long time, he almost comes, says that to her, and then she pulls up from his groin, kisses him on the stomach and chest, bites him on the ear, she wants him to come inside her, but from behind, she gets up in the bed onto her knees and palms, arches her back and shoves her arse towards his crotch. He's behind her now, pressing into her, at first it requires a bit of effort, it pricks the string on the underside of his penis but then it becomes easier. She asks him to spank her, he does, smacks her on the backside, hard, until the skin turns red, he doesn't know if it turns him on or makes him uncomfortable, both, then he grabs her around the hips, pulls her hard towards him. Then he comes. He pulls out again and wipes himself off with a t-shirt.

She lies down on the bed, his semen runs out of her, becomes a patch on the sheet. He wonders if she came, it didn't seem like it, it keeps him awake for a while, they don't speak.

The day after she doesn't want either breakfast or coffee, she has to catch a bus, she says, but kisses him, more sensually than affectionately, on the way out of the door.

15

Over the following days, he thinks a lot about her. He hasn't heard anything. Time goes slowly, he doesn't write anything in particular, just notes down a couple of ideas, things he is thinking about, like being alone in your thirties, it isn't unusual anymore, but what does it mean. The fourth day he sends a text message, she doesn't reply. All these thoughts, how can they not reach their target, doesn't she feel it, that he is thinking about her, wants to talk, to sleep with her again.

He is held hostage by his own phone and its clichés, about waiting. Why doesn't she reply? Does she regret it? Is she aware of the effect it has on him, the strange transitions from hope to disappointment and back to hope? Or, worse: what if she feels used? Could he lose his job, is that what's happening, will he get a call from the boss, what does he do then, what would he say? On the other hand, what if she was using him, a means of harming herself, is that the way she is? Was that why she drew him to her, in an attack of sexual mania, who knows how things work in there, in her head, he doesn't know her well enough, can't draw any conclusions, doesn't know what motivates her. He knows of course who she is, it's not that, at work they refer to her as the "child prodigy," she's the youngest of the staff, writes exceptionally well, is incredibly clever, whip smart, learns quickly. He is fascinated by her, he doesn't hesitate to admit this, to himself, of course, he can't talk about her with their colleagues, not in that way. It's best to appear superior, non-threatened, with respect to a new talent, especially in a work situation, as if you give them (the new talents, that is) too much attention and wish them too much luck, even in conversations where they are not present themselves, it won't take too much for the whole bubble to burst, for the talents themselves too. Not to mention that he would perceive it as awfully embarrassing were someone to realise what he was feeling and thinking about, because what he was feeling and thinking about was not particularly original, he knew that, falling for someone who represents something in one's self, but that no longer exists and which you spend the rest of your life trying to win back. It is no more than five years since he himself was in a similar position, young and so-called promising and the older, more established journalists greeted him with a kind of restraint which was grounded in a genuinely special combination of fear and respect, but also irritation and arrogance. He only just remembers, as it quickly passed; suddenly he was merely one of the staff and not one to keep an eye on, to pay attention to, because his talent was not meaningful in a way that stood out thoroughly or uniquely from others, rather it was the fact that he was so young, actually the youngest to ever write full-time for the newspaper, which was incredible. And when he was no longer young, according to the hectic and ephemeral standards of the world of journalism, then it was no longer something to get excited about, he had become one of the many. He seems to recall experiencing it as a relief when he eventually understood that this was what had happened.

It's Saturday evening, he's drinking beers with Erik, his colleague and best friend, if that's something you can say, again this childishness, why did she have to point that out? It's a week since they slept together, he can't get it out of his head. She's still just as present, even if he hasn't received any answer to his text message and even if he has neither seen nor heard from her in any other way and it is not that he feels stupid, more like powerless, he sees things as for the first time, with her eyes, evaluates what he sees from a completely different angle. The fact that she is in his brain, invisible to him, but just as convincing. He thinks about the power there is in remaining silent, the way she has done over the last week, how it is keeping him trapped in the vague, hazy memories from the night she spent with him, always back to that, since there has not been any change in the image afterwards, no progress, just more of the same. It surprises him that he should have become so obsessed with how she views him, just those minor contours with which she has been presented, what does she think about it, what is it she sees? Or, worse: Does he see the same, does he see it himself?

Erik gesticulates energetically, he is in the middle of a long discourse about the pseudonymous writer Elena Ferrante; the black hairs on his arms stand up straight, as if his own reading of this author gives him goose bumps, he's utterly roused, red in the pudgy face; he is convinced that he has found something in her work that has not been picked up before, it's not so easy to follow, everything seems to sort of stream out of his hands and onto the floor.

Erik is married and has two children; they don't live here, but in Moss, he's bought the apartment in Oslo to be able to work uninterrupted for a couple of weeks every summer without the children, a weekend here and there, and the rest of the year he rents it out. Erik's living room isn't overly inviting; a worn sofa, a leather armchair, everything in dark colours. A bachelor flat, as if to differentiate between dad-Erik and the real or former Erik. Here it has all been recreated, he thinks, this vague feeling of self which does not disappear just because a child steps into your life, it's surely not that simple, even if everything gets suddenly turned on its head, one becomes a machine which exists to serve children, meet the demands which immediately make themselves known in the small bodies and to forget one's own, which are less important. The floor is grubby, the shelves are dusty, sometimes the evenings here become late, that's for sure, whether it is just the two of them or with others, friends and colleagues. That he still likes this kind of room, with emptiness and overcast skies outside, is more than anything else to do with the circumstances connected with these rooms and why he ends up there.

Everything feels easier when Erik is in town, as if the weekdays gain a foothold. They discuss books, politics, sport. They don't talk about Erik's family, in this room there is only space for the big subjects, ideas and theories,

19

occasionally he finds himself thinking that there is something parodic about the way in which they converse, the things that interest them, like football and insipid but realistic left-wing politics, or authors who write about exactly that, he thinks about her again, that she would maybe have laughed at them, but doesn't dare think the thought through, this is what they have together, he and Erik, it is enough. The petty everyday is not their concern.

When does the match start? asks Erik, he turns on the TV.

Half seven, I think.

So there's half an hour to go, says Erik, we'll leave it on until then. He puts the remote control down on the teak table, opens the beer bottles with the help of a snus box. Here, says Erik and hands him a bottle.

By the way, I heard that you and the child prodigy hit it off at the summer party, he says and leans back in the sofa, rests an arm over the edge of it.

So they're talking about it at work, he thinks, it's true, it's not something he has imagined, or dreamt. It really happened. Emilie and he, close to each other at the party, wrapped around each other in the backseat of the taxi on the way home, later in bed, the one meant for only one person. He becomes flushed, wonders if it is visible, if he is reddening.

Emilie and I? Yes, yeah, that's true, as such.

So, do you like her, he asks, or was it a one night thing?

Of course it was a one night thing, he says, Someone had to sleep with the child prodigy sooner or later, it might as well be me.

20

Erik laughs, they both laugh, that's how their relationship is: light, effortless. Oh, how they value each other's cynicism, he thinks. These are the things that unite them.

A child prodigy, is that not pushing it a bit far? It's almost two o'clock at night, he is walking home from Erik's. Normally he takes a taxi, but tonight it's warm, almost suffocating. The conversation with Erik is buzzing in his head, but doesn't lead to anything firm that he can dissect on the way home. Just anecdotes from the job, the working life they share. 'Why is nothing dealt with,' Erik had said. 'The coffee machine, for example, that howls and makes a racket all day.' Sometimes he becomes convinced that the conversations between himself and Erik, even though they are both well-read and quick-witted men, have something indisputably simple about them. He has noticed it in conversations with other men as well, a kind of natural emotional abyss between them. If you heard a similar discussion between two women, on the other hand, you'd possibly think that those women were not all there, mentally speaking.

Should he walk up the street where Emilie lives, just to see, maybe she's been out too, it is a Saturday night, she's young, of course she has been out. Then they run into each other, she on the way home from some bar where she's been with friends, drunk on cocktails, on conversation, he from Erik's, there could be something in it, it would have suited him well now, if she showed up. On the other hand, it would seem suspicious if she found him here, on her street in the middle of the night, if he stumbled across her, it wouldn't look good. He walks over there anyway, up the street where he knows she lives, but he doesn't know more than that, not the number or the building she lives in. That was one of the first things they told one another, in the kitchen at the office, where they lived and what it was like there, they compared their lives in the different streets of the same city, he remembers that he thought that they should be closer to each other, it seemed possible.

But he cannot find her and neither does he know where to look. In a way it's a relief, as what would he have said, his idea was barely thought through, swing by her street on the way home, with a vague hope of running into her, without it really striking him what consequences that could have, or how the conversation would play out, what does he really have to say to her? For all he knows, she could be lying in there now, in one of the apartments along this street, with another man, one who is not so childlike, with a solid job, mortgage and a double bed, a grown man who doesn't need to play at being a grown-up, it occurs to him naturally, he isn't plagued by thoughts of what he should be doing, as an adult. That it should be precisely her to make him aware of his inner child, whom he will not let go, but who defines and restricts him, strikes him of course as ironic. Equally it's what he feels when he sees or thinks about her, that he is not the finished article, in the same way that she is not.

So, he needs to forget her. He knows how it works, what is required. Better than most, he believes, he knows that you can become obsessed with another person, even fall in love with them - he has done so before, with other girls - and at the same time not be in love at all, by making an effort to be occupied with other things. That is the plan and he must write, keep himself busy.

He sits down at the desk in his living room. The old desk chair which he bought at a garage sale in the neighbourhood, the back of which creaks horribly with the slightest movement; he tries to remain in a state of calm, something which makes his body stiff, as if afraid, and that is the reason why he, as long as he has had the job at the paper, at least the last couple of years, has struggled with significant back pain. At times he is almost stunted, at least that is how it feels. Suddenly he is no longer capable of carrying out basic chores, like hanging out the laundry (even if laundry doesn't exactly take up much of his life – almost all the clothes he has are on the same spectrum of tones of grey, which makes it unproblematic to run all of his clothes through the same wash), making food (his largest outgoing recently has been Indian takeaway, the bin is full of the white, small paper cartons) and cleaning the apartment and himself, it's been a long time since his back was strong enough to be in a position to carry out a basic foot wash. But he stays sitting down. On his to-do list there are two book reviews that need to be written and delivered by Tuesday, it's now Saturday, or Sunday really, if he is to be precise, and he should be, but he's tired. He always starts too late, always just before the deadline anguish starts to gnaw, when it is no longer just his back which is trying to break him, but his head, stomach and eyes too. At work he comes across as distant and nonchalant, indifferent, as if work for him was exactly that, work – and not what it really

23

is: the only thing that gives him a sense of meaning, success and happiness, because there is nothing else that gives him any confirmation; no women, no one in his family. So, he should really get on with it. But it's already late into the night, maybe he should go to bed, get a good night's sleep and work full tilt from the morning onwards, or should he stay up all night, take a chance on the alcohol having an effect on him long enough that he doesn't fall asleep at his screen, so that the intoxication will tone down some of the gravity he feels about the work as a critic, create an illusion that the work he does is only for distribution amongst a niche interest group and not a particularly important and enlightening task, the way that he sees it. No, it's best to go to bed, he thinks at last, he's sharper in the mornings, for better or worse, mainly worse.

When the alarm goes off on Monday morning, he doesn't feel anything. A weak light creeps in under the blind, first hitting the edge of the bed and half an hour later forming a stripe on his thigh, he's that pale. He sits up in bed. The morning's sensation of emptiness. That is why he prefers working first thing, as early as four or five, as then nothing can bite at him. At that time it's biology that rules: first he has to piss, then he needs to drink a glass of water, a mild headache often bothers him in the morning, it's because he doesn't drink enough water, and too much beer as well, he knows that, and within an hour of waking he has to eat something before his stomach region starts to tie itself in knots, as he sits trying to concentrate at his desk and it becomes impossible to ignore. He doesn't think about her in these first few hours, that's the best thing about the routine, that he can write. Only after he showers around eight o'clock and for a brief moment looks at his naked body in the full length mirror in the bathroom, does he begin to think of her, what she did with his pale, long and thin body, how the tip of her tongue circled the head of his penis, he might have to masturbate in the shower so as not to get an erection when they both arrive at the paper's office at nine.

She is standing by the coffee machine in the cafeteria. Her back is turned away from the rest of the room, she's dressed in dark blue and black, her hair knotted tightly at her neck. She doesn't seem to consist of anything other than dark curves. He thinks of his own body: thin, angular.

This cold room at the end of the building, grey, but light, a whole wall with double windows on the left wing. Work is hectic as always; harried and caffeine-driven journalists speed walk between desks, offices and the editor, the noise level is unusually high for a Monday, there are arguments about illustrations and cutting unnecessary text, all these egos at the same paper, how is there even room, he doesn't understand, still they always seem to come to some sort of agreement in the end, minutes before everything gets sent to press and the atmosphere turns from tense and electric to resigned and elated about a probably well-crafted and intelligent newspaper. The paper comes out every Friday and since the early 2000s has more than tripled its print run; he is proud to be a part of the paper and what it stands for, giving weight to what he sees as important things: culture, politics, criticism and research.

I guess you'll also want a coffee, right, she says, as if she had already seen through him when he started walking towards her, that he didn't wait until she was gone to get a coffee, that he saw it as an opportunity to be close to her, in spite of the embarrassment, he wonders if it is visible to her.

Yep, it's going to be a long day, he says. He sees her raise her eyebrow slightly, why does he say these things, in that way, it's so banal, the small talk, it's unbearable, he feels hot, the blushing starting to spread under the skin of his

26

face. She sticks a hand in her trouser pocket, he looks at the shape of her hand in her trousers.

Is everything ok, she asks, you look a bit stressed. Her face softens, one corner of her mouth slants almost crookedly towards the right, his right, that something of her is his, no, this is wrong, all of it. The fact that he becomes nervous makes her embarrassingly touched as well, she lets her index finger circle round the edge of the coffee cup, looks at him without blinking.

Sure, it's going fine, he says, just a lot to do.

What is it you're working on now, she asks, without seeming especially interested in the answer, as if the question was born mainly out of a clinical interest for the hopelessness he is showing towards her.

A review of Houellebecq's last book, he says, it's a book that needs handling with caution, at least in these times.

How exciting, she says, I look forward to reading it. See you at the meeting.

She nods to him, lifts the coffee cup in a sympathetic gesture as she walks past him and down to her desk, it's in the office's left wing, it can't be chance, he's thinking, that position, he'll have to make an effort to not stare at her, not look up over the partition every time he gets stuck working on the review, when he wonders if his view of women, especially young women, is influenced by the books he is tasked with reading and reviewing. For example, this French author that he has been busy with over the last week, who, in his usual, provocative manner, is ridiculing the current political climate – in this book, he imagines a France subject to Islamic religion and control,

27

where women lose their right to vote and are thrown out of the universities, where girls as young as fifteen are married away and lose the right to choose how to live their lives. The main protagonist in the book, a man called François, realises that with this politico-religious situation, middle-aged and lonely men such as himself will be in a position to marry as many young women as they wish and when he doesn't resist the adoption of Islam, it's plain and simply because Islam will make his life more comfortable.

At twelve o'clock the culture department holds a meeting. All subjects are to be laid out for the editorial team, to be discussed openly. They sit around a long, oval table, on the table there are bottles of mineral water, plastic cups and a thermos of coffee, a glass bowl with sweets, for those who wish to help themselves, an attempt at creating a constructive, informal atmosphere and he wouldn't say that it doesn't work, it does, but that it should be so simple! He thinks about how the combination of chocolate and coffee has a tendency to create an almost insufferable angst in him, that it is best to stay away from it, he takes a plastic cup and fills it with mineral water. There is also something about the light in here, he thinks, a depressed person would not be able to remain under this sharp, penetrating light for more than five minutes, a light that makes your whole body itch, that makes you tired even if your whole body is pumping with caffeine, which makes you shake and completely diminishes your drive and you have already felt like that for a long time; there is nothing that inspires you any longer, everything you read bores you; everything you see on TV makes you angry, music is no longer of any interest, it completely drains you, splinters your ear canals, everyone on the street is standing in your way, why do they have to walk so slowly and right in front of you as well, without understanding that you are just behind them and want to go faster, past them, it drives you insane, sweating with anger, then that light and the itch gets worse, an itch that will not go away; you never get down to where it really sits and grinds away.

The culture editor opens a window, it is quiet in the room. Everyone has had their fill of whatever they were wanting. Emilie is drinking coffee, winds a lock of hair around her forefinger, studies the strands of hair, maybe she is thinking that she should go to the hairdresser, that it's beginning to look worn. He notices how several strands of hair are stuck together in a bunch, that it looks stiff, as if it could snap, he knows what it is, in any case he thinks he knows, she's holding the stiff bunch between her fingers, sort of pressing on it, it must be semen, a man has ejaculated in her hair before work, or on her chest and then her dark hair has fallen over her chest as she got up, caught in the sticky, wet mass, there is no doubt.

One by one they present their articles, it is clear that as usual this edition of the paper will contain a good deal of cultural material; about the upcoming autumn art season in Sweden, about war crimes against important relics, four book reviews, two exhibition reviews, an interview and an essay. Of all the staff, the art critics are the happiest, he thinks, working for the only newspaper that still prints art criticism, they might be the last of their kind in this country with full time jobs and good salaries, they present their subject with emotion and passion, use the whiteboard, which is otherwise only used for pranks by the other employees, with the proper marker pens they show how they have structured their reviews, the elegant division of artistic theory, external references and their own intuition. Unlike the other journalists, who present their material with the kind of indifference demonstrative of the fact that they would rather have been somewhere else, or at least would rather have written about something else. Himself, he goes quickly through the Houellebecq review, concentrates on the themes and focus of the novel, with the usual feeling that no one was listening, other than the culture editor, of course, who is paid to provide guidance and to comment on their work, it looks like he enjoys the job and when he is done with his rapid run-through of the review, he gets a positive nod from the editor, good work.

Erik picks up the thread from Friday night and continues his line of argument about Elena Ferrante's *My Brilliant Friend*, which he has reviewed for this week's edition; his contribution also gets an approving nod from the editor, something he imagines Erik is not satisfied with given he sees himself as a genius, whilst also waiting for someone to confirm what he already knows, although it does not look likely to happen, at least not at this paper. Next Emilie speaks about her interview with Kjell Askildsen's biographer, a three-page piece that the editor, after Emilie's exemplary (that's the word the editor uses) proposal, announces as front page-worthy. Erik sighs aloud.

Is she sleeping with the culture editor, he finds himself suddenly wondering, and instantly feels ashamed to be thinking along those lines, as if she did not write well enough for the front page, but had to sleep her way to the top, as they say, no, she was more than good enough. She doesn't need him. It's more the culture editor who needs her, considers her as an asset in the otherwise so male-dominated working environment, a so-called breath of fresh air, with new ideas and a firm grip on the contemporary, as if she belongs to something to which the others do not have access and she does, a kind of youthful sphere which the others have long ago left, more or less of their own accord, he thinks, that's how it goes.

The meeting is over, several of the journalists stay in the meeting room to eat lunch, chat and discuss a few things. Oddmund Eriksen, one of the oldest journalists at the paper, turns on the radio, he always wants to listen to P2 in his lunch break. He rarely speaks with the other employees, exchanges just a few words with the editor before sitting down near the end of the table, far from the others, eats a yoghurt which gets stuck on his tongue, spreads to the corners of his mouth.

It's so shitty, says Erik as he takes a large bite of a shop bought baguette, the salad leaves squeeze out of the baguette under the pressure from his hands, land silently on the napkin.

What's that?

Emilie. That an interview with Askildsen's biographer, not even Askildsen himself, but the biographer, winds up on the front page, says Erik.

No, right enough. Maybe she's sleeping with him too. The editor, I mean.

Him too? What do you mean, are you still sleeping with the child prodigy? asks Erik, wipes his face with the same napkin, a piece of salad gets stuck in his beard.

No, that's not what I meant, but maybe it's a strategy she has. Not a particularly inventive strategy, true, but that sort of thing never quite goes out of fashion, does it?

Who knows, says Erik, it's shitty either way. He swallows down the last bite of the baguette before he gets up and takes a refill of coffee from the thermos. Anyway, back to work, he says and clears his throat, walks out of the room.

He doesn't see her the rest of the day. On the tram on the way home he is angry. The anger is not directed at anything concrete, it is in any case not clear to himself where it comes from. Maybe it's a more general dissatisfaction with everything that is repeating itself in his life, the same story with girls, the fact that he uses the word girls at all, when it should be women, it's not his habit to check out young women, to check out anyone at all, when he thinks about it and he has more than enough time to think here, in the tram on the way home, he should sleep a bit, gather his strength for making dinner or something, he eats too many slices of bread, that's to say the anger is directed at himself, the state of "things." He sends Erik a text message, asks if he fancies getting a beer later, a delayed payday beer, makes clear that it's the beer that's late and not payday, but it's not an especially funny comment, neither was it meant to be, just a clarification, why does he have to be like this? But he already feels some relief, knows that Erik will say yes, it's not often he refuses an invitation that involves alcohol, he cannot remember that Erik has ever said no to that, that's also a kind of comfort, he thinks.

They meet at the Japanese bar which is situated about halfway between their apartments, they have to walk ten minutes from each side, so they are in the middle, it's a good solution. Erik orders sake and edamame beans, for himself he orders potato medallions with teriyaki sauce, he hadn't had time to eat dinner. They drink sake from glasses that look more like cups; thick, black cups made of ceramic and without handles, they are apparently called ochoko, the waitress tells them. The drink tastes acidic, almost like a dry and clear white wine. He looks around the room, doesn't manage to concentrate on the conversation with Erik, he's looking for Emilie, maybe she's here, it isn't unimaginable, she goes out a lot, he has realised, the long body, the shoulder-length brown hair. He lets his gaze move from table to table, all the backs, necks, imagine if he saw her here, with her arm around another man's back, maybe the boss, no one knows what can happen. He does not see her.

Erik gesticulates as he always does, it's not so easy to keep up, and neither does he try, everything is just chaos. Do you not agree, asks Erik with a firm grip around the sake cup and raising his eyebrows in expectation.

Yes, of course, he answers. Hopes that he does, he isn't one of those who struggles to argue with Erik, there are many, indeed, who allow themselves to be persuaded or scared off by how single-minded he is, that in itself is convincing enough, that cocksureness, but personally he is not one of them.

Are you looking for someone, or…? asks Erik.

Me? No, I'm just checking out the room, he says. The boss apparently comes here, I heard.

Right. Did you hear about Emilie by the way?

What about Emilie?

There we go, now you've woken up, says Erik. Well, she got a new job offer, at a publishing house.

At a publisher, he says, right, well, is she going to take it then? He feels heavy, the thought of not seeing her every day, by the coffee machine in the morning, the brief conversations that leave him in an ecstatic state of despair for the rest of the day.

Seems like it, it's a good role, an editorial job. No doubt more exciting and better paid than at the paper, says Erik.

Who did you hear about it from?

She told Siri, says Erik. After lunch, I was stood by the coffee machine and overheard their conversation.

He wants to go home. The disappointment is so massive and so heavy that he cannot manage to get up. Erik asks if he fancies a proper drink, he says yes, as he does want one after all, he doesn't have any spirits at home. Two sake sours on the table. Later Japanese whisky. He wants to go home, he feels like crying. The alcohol puts pressure on the insides of his eyeballs, they must be red by now, but he cannot cry, that won't do. He looks at Erik. Large, powerful hands, his fingers are long with wide fingertips, nails. He is quite solid, generally, Erik, a grown man. Personally, he is lacking backbone, he thinks, power of judgment, falling in

34

love with girls whom he hopes will give him confirmation, in various ways, both sexually and intellectually, he thinks dejectedly. Because he is so awkward, both physically and socially, it's easier with younger women, he tells himself, usually it gives him a sense of calm being around them, a self-assuredness purely based on the fact that he has a few years on them and this to his advantage, but with her it is different – she is like a mirror set up in front of his body, he sees himself as just one long bone, one that does not know where it begins and far less where it ends. Without reason, only with feelings, he considers the defeat which his love life must appear to be, to Erik and all the others, it's not so difficult to imagine. But he does have friendship, he values that, in his youth it was all he wanted, now he has it, he and Erik, they sit up late on the summer evenings, talk low and easily together. That's also why Erik notices what is bothering him, that there is a pained expression on his face, vaguely apologetic, and he asks him, is everything alright, but doesn't dig more than this, which is almost the minimum, as his closest friend.

He looks down at the table and between his hands sees that his drink is almost empty, he is about to order a new one when Erik yawns, stretches out his arms, says that it is probably time to go home, it is a work day tomorrow after all. They wave the waitress over and ask for the bill, pay separately and go out into the summer night, it's raucous, noise and shouts everywhere, music, bass from the apartments around them. Bloody hell, says Erik, rubs his eyes. They give each other a clap on the shoulder as they part ways on the pavement, see you tomorrow. On the way home, all alone and with no battery on his phone, he thinks that maybe it's the alcohol, but it's as if he can hear how the close, warm air almost absorbs all the noise, how everything is packed in.

The next day he gets to work extra early. He hasn't had much sleep, maybe a couple of hours and when he brushes his teeth in the staff toilets he sees the bags under his eyes, he doesn't look good, he's worn out, so unbelievably worn out and broken, his thin hair is wet and sits as if stuck to his skull. He straightens his back, looks at the scrawny, weak figure he cuts, thinks that he should start running again. He used to be quite active, his body felt firm and tight against the mattress at night, he suspects that it was really effective for emptying the mind, as they say, that you can run from some things. But now he doesn't have the energy, or the desire, just the idea of changing into training gear and running through town on hard pavement, no, it would weigh heavily on his day, the knowledge that he would have to go out and run after work, it's too much, too dark.

He gets himself a coffee from the communal kitchen. The light in there isn't as sharp as elsewhere in the office, some of the pressure in his head is released, it's cool and pleasant, not to mention the smell of coffee, these are the best minutes of the day, he thinks, when he stands there waiting for the coffee, all alone, when it's calm at work and there is still a cold breeze coming through the windows, it feels good. Standing at the counter he eats a slice of bread with butter, he doesn't feel so bad, almost happy, but also with the knowledge that this good feeling is normally limited to these few minutes in the morning and that the disappointments will have their turn later, he is without question a morning person, at his quickest and most malleable then, when everything still feels new and almost hopeful, before the day wears him down, if he is honest and his mood follows it, he becomes bad-tempered, it makes him think about what else could have been, even if it is of little benefit, really quite pointless to think like that, he knows it and when he goes to bed just before midnight, he'll be completely drained of energy, or so-called lust for life, can only hope to get to sleep and that the sleep will act as a portal to the next morning, back to that small glint of meaning and happiness that will strike him.

He worked solidly for the next hours, he ends up being satisfied with the review, it is well worked, his reflections are unusually good, he thinks, well balanced, he has taken the writer's project seriously, but also seen the problematic side of certain passages in the book, without being too moralising or, heaven forbid, politically correct, it is not a boring or predictable article, on the contrary he has succeeded in opening up to a range of interpretations, covered several interesting questions about gender, race and the political leanings of the novel, it's all in all a genuinely constructive piece of criticism, he thinks, maybe some of his best work for the paper, it's almost a shame the author himself will never read the review. But he is missing a title. Maybe he can ask Emilie, she will no doubt read his article if she has time, it's a good way to get closer to her, he thinks; innocent.

She is sitting at her desk, looks concentrated and impenetrable, as she usually does, he thinks. He has seen another version of her, undisguised and open, at this moment it is almost inconceivable to think that he has seen her naked, no, had her naked in front of him, in his bed in his own apartment. That he has felt her tits press against his own chest, it feels strange, distant.

Should he really bother her with this, he thinks, but still walks over to her, his body softly pulsing and throbbing, not unlike the feeling that comes with the day's fourth cup of coffee, how many has he actually drunk today, it must be a fair few, and now, a kind of "nervous protest" as he stops in front of where she sits, absorbed in work, before she realises that he is standing there, expectantly. She takes the earphones out of her ears, he wonders what she is sitting listening to, what kind of music she likes, for example, or is she listening to something else, a podcast maybe. What are you listening to, he asks, but regrets it, maybe that's too intimate a question, here at the office, although he is here in a professional context, it is safe.

White noise, she says, it helps me concentrate. He nods, goes quiet, has almost forgotten what he came over here for, becomes engrossed in her and everything that makes her possible. She turns towards him, but only with her upper body, as if she is required to sit with her legs crossed, knee over thigh, with one hand in her lap and the other resting, but occasionally active and engaged, on the keyboard; only her back is turned toward him. Did you want something, she asks and pushes her hair behind her ear.

Yes, he says. Sorry to bother you, I could just use a little help, you know, I'm more or less done with the review but

39

can't come up with a good title, it's not really my strong suit, but maybe you're good at it? Could you take a look, do you think, see if a good title springs to mind?

I'm rambling, he thinks, not exactly my strong suit, why does he talk like that, such a loser. He seems in his own eyes to be almost painfully transparent, it is as if he sees what she sees, which is after all the closest you can come to another's view of yourself.

Yes, I guess so, she says, not sure if I'll be much help, but I can have a bit of a look after I've filed my interview for proofing. Just send me an email with the article, she says and smiles. A small wave of disorientation falls over him, he stays standing there for a few seconds, sees her pop the earphones back in and that they stay sitting like small buttons in her ear canals, now he cannot stay there much longer; he snaps out of it, says thanks. She can't hear him. He walks back to his desk.

At 15.04 her name comes up on his screen, an email. 'Looks fine. Should we get that beer this evening, by the way? Nine o'clock?'

He leaves home early. He read somewhere that lustful men often look like dogs at the moment when their owner gets the lead out for a walk. He has rolled up his shirt sleeves, the hairs on his arms are fair, like a woman's, he thinks, or a young boy's, and he has freckles over his wrists. He buys a beer, sits at the back of the bar, in the middle of an empty set of sofas, the leather makes a muted squeaking noise as he crosses his right leg over his left.

40

There are things about her that he doesn't like. There must be and he tries to think about them now before she comes, he cannot keep putting her on a pedestal, needs to bring her back down again, make her human, for it to be possible for them to have a normal conversation, he is older than her after all, knows more. He doesn't like how she, especially when in more intellectual company than at work, at a party for the culture sections, or at a completely ordinary bar for that matter, so long as the guests are important and interesting enough, especially the older, successful men, tries the whole time to drive the conversation towards her own young age, that she is so unbelievably young, and to thus fish for compliments or recognition of her impressive intellect, the work she does, or just the way she discusses and converses, so introspective and mature, in spite of her age. There is without doubt something deceiptful about how she presents herself, he thinks, he cannot be the only one to have noticed this, it's actually a sign of deep uncertainty, isn't it, that she is so dependent on approval from her superiors? But this just makes him feel more sympathetic towards her and to be the one who gives that approval. In other words, this line of thought has backfired.

He cannot give her too much affirmation, he knows that, then she would be done with him pretty quickly, it has to be just enough and he also needs to vary his compliments to show that he sees things in her that others have not picked up on earlier, so that she comes back for more.

He has thought a lot about this recently, the methodical side of love. If it is possible to influence, even manipulate, the other's feelings with the help of some basic, psychological principles. Anything else makes no sense, he thinks. Even if it is difficult to pretend to be unaffected, it's just as hard to play normal, both friends and acquaintances can easily see how feelings well up in someone at the mere mention of the name of the object of their desires, maybe it is still possible to force yourself to, manipulate yourself to displaying some form of indifference. To put your brain on ice until the point where something changes. He thinks that he has an advantage, namely that he is so reserved, also just in his own company, that the chances of him bringing her name up in conversation in a clumsy and unconvincing manner are low. He thinks about the game. He is naturally anxious that she will play with him, he imagines that women are better at that kind of psychological contortion and he is convinced of his own weakness, his susceptibility. For now he is the weaker party, the one who feels and wants the most; that is easy to exploit. Something he read yesterday, which completely absorbed his attention, was a lengthy article about the push and pull phenomenon, a kind of method of attraction which consists of one party, presumably the stronger, constantly ensuring they are interacting with the other in some way, so that the strong party at any time can switch between pushing the other away and pulling him toward them; every time the other is upset by the lack of consideration and affirmation and is starting to pull out of the relationship, the strong party will put out a small piece of bait, a short phone conversation or a light and noncommittal hand on his shoulder, which will prove to be sufficient attention that he continues making himself available to her. He is afraid that this is how she thinks and operates, of course he is, even if it is only hypothetical and not necessarily something she has particularly thought about, the way he has, now.

She arrives ten minutes late. She waves to him from the bar while she buys a beer, doesn't appear to be in a hurry and when she comes over to him with the glass in her hand, she doesn't apologise, but she is in a good mood, and looks great too, it's as if she has got dressed up for him. Hi, she says. All well?

Yes, everything fine here, he says. I'm happy you wanted to meet.

She sits down, takes a couple of quick sips of her beer, smiles at him, pushes her hair behind her ear, it's something she does often. You look nice, he says.

I liked your review, she says. Of course I haven't read the book you've written about, but I could see that it was a good read, it made me interested.

Thanks, he says. I'm glad you think so, I spent a while on it.

He would so much like to freeze this moment, were it possible, that the two of them could sit here in something he can only describe as some kind of "forever," but he knows that it doesn't work like that and he becomes embarrassed, catching himself thinking like a lovestruck fourteen year old girl.

So, she says. Today was my last day at the paper.

Are you done already?

Yes, I begin at the publishers on Monday, she says. Some hair falls down into her face, this time she doesn't adjust it,

43

lets it hang down her cheek, a few strands of hair get stuck in her eyelashes, he wants to fix it, cannot.

Well. Are you looking forward to it then?

I really am, she says, it feels right. It's kind of a dream job if the expression isn't too daft.

It's not, he says. So why did you want to meet me now?

Just for a last beer, she says. We won't see each other much after all, at least not day to day. You were the only one I really wanted to say goodbye to.

It sounds serious, he says. As if you were moving to another country.

Yes, she says and laughs, I'm actually just going to the other side of the street.

But I'm glad you wanted to, he says, still unsure of what it is she wants with him, it's far from clear, is she thinking of sleeping with him, to get some kind of closure to it all, whatever "it all" is, he certainly doesn't know, it's her who is driving this.

There's also that I have just realised, well the past week, that you actually quite like me, she says, smiles.

Well, yes, you're right, he says. Is that why you wanted to meet me now, to console your lonely, older colleague who has fallen in love with you?

Ex-colleague she says.

Ex-colleague. That's true.

No, it's nothing like that, she says. I really like you. But I have a boyfriend.

You have, he says. How long?

A little over a year now.

Does he know about us, he asks and immediately regrets the use of the word "us," there is no them, he knows that of

44

course, almost painfully well and now he comes across as full of illusions as to what their one night together meant.

No, she says simply. And he won't find out about it either, there is no point. It was about sex, nothing else, in any case as far as I was concerned. So I'm sorry if I gave you another impression. I was acting on impulse.

I get it, he says. It's fine, really.

Yes, she says, as if it were a question.

Absolutely, he says. Do you want another beer, he asks and points at the empty glass in front of her, as if nothing of what she has said has really sunk in and it probably hasn't, part of him knows this, lets it pass.

I don't know if that's such a good idea, she says.

Come on, it's not so dangerous, surely we can celebrate that you have got a new job?

Yes, she says, drags it out a little. When you put it that way. I'd love a beer, she says.

He gets up and goes over to the bar, sees in the mirror by the door that she is taking out her mobile, quickly typing with her fingers, maybe a text to her boyfriend, he's probably waiting for her and she is waiting to go home to him but is still sitting here, out of sympathy for her sad, pathetic and lonely colleague, she must think he is quite ridiculous.

Here, he says and hands her the beer. She thanks him, looks a little uncomfortable sitting with her hands in her lap so she crosses her arms, looks almost sternly at him, challenging him. What are you thinking about, he asks, but she just shrugs slightly and because he realises that an actual reply to the question would scare him, he doesn't insist but instead grasps his beer glass, empties it, looks round the bar, while her stare doesn't let go of him, is fixed there, on something, he almost does not dare think about what it is she is seeing. She probably sees how uncomfortable he is, that he's sweating, that the glass only just avoids slipping out of his clammy hand, why did he want this, what had he imagined?

I should probably go, she says after a while and puts the empty glass down on the table.

Yes?

But this was, she says and pauses, well, nice. Guess I'll see you around.

She puts her coat on, walks over to him and kisses him on the cheek then rests the palm of her hand there, against his cheek, looks at him, it's all quite intense, he manages to think in the few seconds that they stare right at each other and she leans over and kisses him, her tongue, it lasts a moment, the whole bodily alarm system is activated, there is a tightening in his groin, he wants to put a hand around her, on her backside, pull her into him, but then she pulls away again, clearly bothered by the situation but smiling at least, almost jokingly, before she walks away from him.

He stays sitting for a couple of minutes, tries to consider everything that has happened from a point somewhere above his own head, and whatever it is, from now on it has no meaning, he thinks, he can neither fight or argue against it, hardly even feel it, in any case not as anything more than a small comma in his lasting story as a desirous man, one who in a way is trying, even if only for these few years until he no longer feels "vital" and by that he means potent, to get closer to her, the comma.

EXCESS IN SEPTEMBER

She stands out in the middle of a black and warm carpark, gleaming cars and yellow stripes, white stripes. She cannot remember where she has parked the car. While she looks for it, she thinks about what her psychiatrist said in there. He asked her to take pills for the things that made her unhappy. His smell is sharp and confidence inspiring, she can't describe it as anything other than sweet and salty at the same time and the sweet makes him attractive, the salt makes her respect him, even if she is unsure if salt, which is after all something you primarily taste, is also something you can smell, but that's how he comes across, positively.

She reluctantly tells him about her childhood, only because he asks about it. Personally she doesn't believe it is of importance, in no way explanatory, as to what is happening and what she sees as being her problem. It's no doubt a part of the so-called program he has put together, not just for her, but for everyone who sees him. Not about the whole of childhood, of course, nor about that which could be considered to be the most important, namely the parents, attachment and so on, but about brief glimpses from childhood's loneliness, those moments when her parents were not around; not due to a failure in their duty of care or anything like that, just those few hours in the afternoon when she finished early at school and they had not yet come home from work. She tells him about the burning shame. The arm of the sofa between her legs. How

48

she rubbed herself back and forth on it, with the upper part of her genitals pressed against the rough cloth, first slowly, then quickly and intensely, before it all culminated in a swelling and uncontrollable feeling which in a way was the opposite of pain, but with the same intensity, which she would later learn was climax, an orgasm, she was ten years old, all she knew was that it felt good, that there had to be something wrong with her, that it had to be kept a secret; the pleasure swiftly turned into something unpleasant which almost made it not worthwhile, with the stuff that ran out of her and became cold on the inside of her thighs, on the edge of the sofa.

The car is over in the far corner of the carpark. She parks as far away from other cars as possible. But just on the other side of her a shining and, from what she can tell, expensive car, red and spotless, one of those cars where the roof goes down at the push of a small button, a cabriolet, it was already here when she parked. When she goes up to the door of her own car and takes out the key to unlock it, she turns quickly, the whole thing happens on impulse; she touches the tip of the key against the paintwork of the red car, presses down and scratches a shiny, horizontal stripe from the handle of the front door to the handle of the rear door. Then she stares at her work for a few seconds before she catches sight of the car owner running towards her, he's shouting something, she moves quickly, hurriedly brushes off the key and tries to unlock her car, thinks over the course of these few milliseconds about the nightmares from when she was a child, when she was always running from something, like a monster, or a sinister man, but was somehow never able to open the door that would enable her to escape the situation, or her legs would be struck with a sudden rheumatism, she would be rooted to the spot, but this wasn't a dream, the car door opens, she gets in and turns the key, hears the car owner shout *cunt* as she drives out of the carpark, *fucking cunt*, he shouts again, she swings out onto the main road, shaking in the driver's seat. Hopes he didn't see the license plate.

There is a rhythm in everything she does, she thinks, like breathing, something machinelike and automatic about the way she appears to other people, a kind of restraint which comes across as cynicism more than shyness, she is angry, so incredibly angry and this is not the first time that strangers have suffered because of it. Only when it comes to sex, she thinks, is it different: here she adapts, is open to things, is present. She has a voluptuous body, like a fruit, light skin and thick hair, that sort of thing goes noticed, she's made for it. The soft bend of her hips, some call it a curved body, she is curvaceous, they say, personally she considers her body to be exaggerated, consisting of troughs and bulges, that this makes it valuable; it has its own currency. She often describes her body in the third person, as if she too sees it as an object and not an actual, important part of her, but as a kind of tool, heavy and effective. She becomes sad, when she acknowledges this. It makes her unbelievably sad to think like that.

The day she gathered together her things from the office, just two months after she had started the new job, she noticed, as she reached for a book on the top shelf, that her arms were covered in red, dry patches, the ones that usually showed up when she had slept too little or was stressed. It's one of those things that you don't notice until you suddenly do. Like with spiders. Like with everything.

It was the book manuscripts, she thought, which had to be read and evaluated, that she didn't have the strength for, nor any real interest in, not necessarily because the quality was poor, but because she couldn't tell them apart from one another – literature by consensus, written by men in their thirties, lost loves, clumsy dialogue, affectations. It wasn't that the content surprised her, on the contrary, it was as expected, but she failed to muster any empathy for it, how such trivialities were blown up. She didn't recognise the characters, didn't believe in them – common to the many male authors was an obvious simplicity of view of the whole female condition, her breasts, her figure, blah blah. That this pubescent, physical expression of the female characters was followed by overblown declarations of love that pretended to be grounded in something more than straightforward erotic fascination, made the whole thing seem even more absurd. She just shredded them without discussing with the head of publishing, or with anyone else for that matter, let the fragments of paper slip through her hands, threw them carefully up into the air before they landed in her hands again. They must have been so hopeful, she thought, when they printed out and posted their thick manuscripts, many of them had doubtless spent several years on it, maybe this was what they were counting on, and now they lay there, in millions of small pieces in front of her. She slept in work hours, used the keyboard as a pillow, ground up Ritalin pills in the staff toilets and snorted them with the assistance of the key card she had hanging around her neck, drank coffee and Red Bull until the letters on the paper looked like barcodes.

She learns that chances can sink inwards, like a bathtub slowly emptying. She of course understood that there was something wrong, but exactly what it was, where it came from, that her eyes seemed to sink back in her skull and made it impossible to focus on anything, neither faces nor letters or road signs, that she didn't manage to look forward to anything, that which had previously given her energy and pleasure was suddenly gone, she didn't know what it was or how such a thing could happen.

Once, a long time ago, when she was eleven or twelve, in a unisex toilets at a service station at the side of the motorway, she saw a man rubbing his own penis, quickly, as if he was trying to pull it off his body altogether, and around him, on the walls, childish and vulgar drawings of genitals, rude words, thought and written by anonymous hands:

COCK AND PUSSY TOGETHER FOREVER
MARTIN FUCKED JOHANNA HERE (12.07.1998)

The man caught sight of her where she stood looking at him, but didn't stop, carried on while he watched her, almost smiling, as if having a witness to his self-embrace made it more important, erotically important, he was no longer just embracing himself and maybe she looked scared, horrified by all these simultaneous impressions, or just sad that the change had to happen so quickly, but that was not how it was, she stared back, fascinated, aroused. Suddenly her lack of shyness became a problem, he probably thought that she was sick, hadn't expected her to stay standing there, watching him. Go away, he said, and she went.

She spends her days on the balcony, drinking coffee, reading newspapers or books, the radio humming from the living room. But today it's raining, she is wearing an anorak, rain drops run down the blue hood, so heavily that it seems as if they might seep through the material. Like a head massage, she thinks, closes her eyes and smokes a cigarette, she only needs one every day, in the morning just after she gets up.

In the place where she exists it is calm and quiet. Wind, the radio, occasional rain, like now, but no real noise – no time, other than that which she herself can conceive of, that she controls. She is from time to time quite happy, that she can say, she is at least comfortable in her own company, it's in relation to others that the problems arise, or that is exactly when her complicated relationship with herself is heightened, rendered visible, further complicated.

That she lives alone in this way, even young as she is, and resourceful too, relatively pretty, not sensationally beautiful or anything like that, but cute at least, that this is a way of living. That she walks around in here, in a kind of obscurity, almost in a haze, without having anyone to talk about it to, whatever it is, and without asking about anything, that she's so strange. Her first (and only) boyfriend said that to her: You are strange. And it's true, she sometimes has completely insane thoughts, like: 'I think my leg is my father's tail' and so on, but then that's why she goes to therapy, because of thoughts like these, she doesn't understand why it had to bother him.

She often thinks of him, the ex-boyfriend, still, but almost only sexually. First and foremost because she really struggles to remember it, how they slept together, what he looked like naked, what they did. She can remember that he was like most other young men, selfish, not much interested in anything other than his own orgasm; it always hurt a little when she guided him in, she usually went on top, it didn't last long, he made an almost hostile face when he came. He was just two years older than her and they were together for around the same time, so for a while. She remembers the distance he kept between them, even when they were a couple, he rarely called, never sent messages – for him it was enough to meet once a week. So maybe that was it, the arrogance he displayed to her, that he was so indifferent, she wanted him to own her. At that point in her love for him, if she can call it that, she tried to make herself look nice, to find ways to be more gentle and delicate, before it became clear that she was immovable, fixed. That she was already a person, that something in her was set, that was how she experienced it. She cut her fringe in order to make changes, the strands of hair crackled as the scissors created an opening around her face. Around him she was normal, and in fact was superior to him, he didn't challenge her on an intellectual level, he was certainly intelligent, but it didn't always come out that way.

One evening, just a week after she had seen him for the first time, she sits wrapped in a blanket in his living room. It's evening and winter, he comes up to her and sticks his hand in under the blanket, which she does not consider as unusual, they are close from the beginning, what does almost scare her however, is that he completely without warning drives his hand up between her legs and grabs hold and that she can neither get up or move away from the hand's grasp around her crotch and that she instead turns her head towards the right with her cheek turned away from him, in an attempt to remove herself (with her eyes) from the situation. It is a kind of action so insane that it is almost as if it never happened, even if it did, even if she is almost certain of it. When he releases his grip and she eventually gathers herself, she kisses him carefully on the ear and the whole thing becomes even stranger as he doesn't show her any kind of affection, on the contrary the kiss seems almost to confuse him and suddenly she thinks that it is her own fault. She knows that it is not, but that is how he makes her feel, her distrust is nothing compared to his matter-of-factness, he looks embarrassed on her behalf and embarrassed on his own behalf for even breathing the same air as her.

She doesn't feel as if she is seen, not really, so she sees others. She goes out with friends, they drink, they meet men, she goes home with them. Not because she wants to, she doesn't think, but because they touch her and see her and give her compliments. It's weak, almost animalistic, she thinks, to not be able to grab the problem by the root, as they say, but instead just putting a plaster over the wound, other men as plasters.

The entrance to his apartment is inviting and it's actually she who finds it for him, he takes over the lease when her best friend moves to Copenhagen and she is at least as fond of the living room, which is decorated in an old fashioned manner and so is cosy in its own particular way, like coming home to grandma's for dinner, she thinks, with all the tenderness that implies. And that she never gains any perspective on the act that becomes their relationship, or on what led up to that act, will make it even worse afterwards, as she sees it: that the memories sometimes spring up without warning, when she is brushing her teeth or taking out the rubbish, and immediately make her anxious, full of longing and guilt and even if the medication has to a certain extent muted these unbearable feelings, they are still just as present; she realises that these feelings are something that she must live with, maybe for the rest of her life, and that they are in fact deserved, a fitting punishment for the pain she has caused him.

It is possible that these events come back in short glimpses because they are of a kind she doesn't understand herself, in the sense that she doesn't know what she is doing at that moment and the sight of his hurt and agonised face when she tells him everything, about the other men, is all that remains as an actual memory.

You could maybe say that when these "episodes" hit her, it is the feeling of a kind of earthquake of the soul and everything becomes twisted, like her own perception of herself as a "person," that is to say a being with a sense of morals and an understanding of vulnerability.

On the underground, young women with soft skin, the scent of soap, their faces are a domino-row of self-awareness, she thinks, there's always something that needs to be adjusted: hair, makeup, sitting position, one leg crossed over the other. Every woman is her own continuous improvement project. They stare straight ahead, with exactly the same pained look on their faces. She relaxes, everything seems normal. Men look at her as she is used to, maybe she appears accessible, she meets their gaze with calm and self-confidence. If she wants, she can have them. Many young women are not aware of how easy it is.

She stands on the balcony and freezes, her hair is wet, she has slept too little the past week, can feel it, plus she has been crying even if that is not something that is a habit and her eyes almost hang down, pulling on her face. Pathetic, she thinks. Not irregularly she feels as though her own emotional existence is a source of embarrassment, of soul searching; she has a kind of delusion of grandeur, a belief that she is too intelligent to have the same unoriginal feelings as everyone else, at the same time she feels ashamed of this arrogance.

One and a half pills. She swallows the whole one first, then splits the other with a kitchen knife, presses down on the stripe in the middle and swallows that half too. She dreams a lot. For several months there have been dreams unlike those from before: hectic and throbbing and as if completely distanced, with detours and falls from great heights, she awakes with a start at night, feels the small shocks of nerves and feelings from somewhere deep inside. Then she wakes to the light pushing in around the sides of the blinds, which don't fully cover the windows and there, on her body, there are large red patches which itch and burn along her arms and across her stomach, the psychiatrist says it's a reaction to stress and even if she knows that, recognises it, she can hardly believe him; that something that comes from so deep inside her can proliferate in that way, on the outer layer of her skin.

The woman in the health food shop always says hello with the palms of her hands pressed together, arms up towards her face, *Namasté*. She nods back, walks along the shelves to make it clear that she wants to shop alone. She picks up toothpaste, a couple of bars of soap and a bar of chocolate.

The woman puts these purchases in a paper bag at such an unhurried tempo that it almost drives her completely nuts, as if this is where her human pride lies and when she, on top of this, smiles in a rather satisfied manner as she very slowly folds down the top of the bag, the whole thing becomes even stranger. Totally ruined by the slow living movement, she thinks, tries to look past the woman, out to the street, over to the other side, she doesn't want to encourage her.

Anything else I can help with? the woman asks and lifts her head carefully towards her, her voice provocatively bright, insincerely friendly.

I want to start a diet, she says.

Oh really? You don't look like you need to lose weight.

I want to shrink.

The health food shop woman gives her a brochure with information about a course of so-called "plant based" dieting, she feels that she has to thank her. On the way out she stops in the doorway, turns, says *Namasté to you too*. Not really for any reason in particular.

In the evening she runs into Espen. She has not seen him since the time they had a last beer together as colleagues, it's six months ago now. They say hi to one another in a bar in the west end of town. Now that they meet each other here, she thinks that it is unclear what brought them together in the first place, other than the obvious, that they worked at the same paper, that evening she went home with him, what came over them then. They talked about how much alcohol there was at that party, but where did the attraction come from? Espen still works at the newspaper, she asks him to tell her what has changed on the editorial team since she left.

He doesn't appear to be bitter, a little reserved perhaps, but happy to see her again. He talks easily, not about how she suddenly cut contact. At some point, she thinks, all of the crazy things she did must have blindly come together in his conscious; that she more or less disappeared, the cheating that she made him a part of, the game. The way she stroked her fingers over his shoulder one minute, before she became cold, indifferent in the next. Eventually, little by little, maybe he has forgotten about it.

Oddmund died a few months ago. Otherwise there is not much news, he says and hesitates a little, as if he is unsure about whether to tell her any more, if it would be appropriate. But we have got a new staff member, she's a young woman too, a couple of years older than you, he says. She reminds me a bit of you actually, with dark, short hair. I spoke to her for the first time a couple of days ago, she told me about something absurd that had happened to her on the way to work for her first day. She had been running along the street because she was late out the door and after just a few hundred metres she suddenly ran into an old teacher from primary school, whom she at this point hadn't seen for probably twenty years and who insisted she should stop and talk to him, as if she owed him that much after almost knocking him over and when she told him that she had got a job at our paper, he had shaken his head, stared into her eyes for what felt like several minutes and said with disappointment in his voice: I was so sure that you would become a vet. Strange, right?

She is silent, answers with a smile, realises that it is best if she just listens, doesn't speak, as she is still not sure what brought her here, with Espen in front of her. She wonders if he is trying to make her jealous, or to show that she is replaceable, as she thinks it is working, a little at least. There is something painful about the thought of the new girl, she feels it clearly when he talks about her, she can't help wondering if he has slept with her, tries to imagine it, but cannot, that helps.

What about you, are you still with your boyfriend, he asks. Meaning she must break her silence.

No, she says, it came to an end.

Did he find out about us?

It was because of a few things, she says.

A few men? he asks probingly. That he dares, she thinks.

Something like that.

63

How about the new job?

That came to an end too, she says, not without smiling a little, as she is worried about being seen as pretentious.

He doesn't ask any more. It's about building up complicated structures that can allow me to live with it, she thinks, doesn't say. By 'it' she means the unhappiness she passes on to others, not just Espen, but herself, other men and which she has to live with, which cannot be wiped out afterwards. That she disappears, uses and rejects. She is sure that she will never bring it up again. She doesn't wish any harm to anyone, she knows that and it is not as if she completely believes that Espen has no recollection of what happened between them, but when she thinks about it, it is possible that he has repressed it. Without being certain about it she may appear somewhat conceited, she thinks, but then neither is it true that she is not aware of this, how she always puts herself first. Is that not the duty of mankind?

When they have sat opposite each other for a while, she feels an urge to seduce him, subtly, so that he can make the first move. Her manner changes, is no longer witty and reflective, she makes herself malleable, withers in front of him. Even if he, she is quite convinced, sees her as more intelligent than himself, it doesn't take much for him to get a hard-on. She rubs it with her hand, outside his clothes. She thinks that he probably hasn't slept with anyone since that time they did it, it's both a sickening and an arousing thought, how much he wants her, he's thought about this, she can see it in his face, how his mouth carefully opens,

64

his eyes don't meet hers but instead focus completely on the enjoyment, he wants to see it, his own cock under his trousers, what she's doing with it.

They go back to his place, continue in the bedroom. When they get there, she no longer wants to be malleable. Instead she becomes commanding, not in a way that scares him, at least that is not the intention, but she exerts a kind of dominating behaviour, like how she doesn't let him touch her, gently slaps his hands away if he tries, she wants to see him jerk off in front of her, as if she wasn't there, she tells him. She maybe comes across as dominating, she thinks, without being able to say that it has anything to do with some kind of participation in an absurd sexual ideology, it's always on impulse. She watches while he carries out the muscular movements with his hand, and something sort of trembles inside her, soon she'll interrupt, she rubs herself back and forth over a bunching of the duvet. He does what she says, she tells him to hold firmly under the head of his penis so that he doesn't come yet, they are not finished. He pauses, looks at her, His cock points towards the pot plant on the windowsill on the left side of the room.

Can I touch you now, he asks.
No, she says and begins to touch herself, she lies on her back on the bed and stretches her legs almost carefully towards the ceiling, rocks back and forth.

Let me touch you, he says.
Wait.

She doesn't feel obliged to let him have her, so she doesn't
let him have her.

There are several reasons, says the psychiatrist; he talks about her general distrust in men, which in turns leads to men's general distrust of her. She speaks about her father, how she studied him when she was little, when she walked past the bathroom under the stairs, he stood there shaving slowly. Her mother outside in white gardening gloves, on her knees in front of a plant, the name of which she did not know, outside the kitchen window, just in front of her where she stood pouring a glass of water.

She told him long ago that she had had a good upbringing, it's not by talking about her childhood that he was going to tease out some kind of final breakthrough, she doesn't believe that. There was nothing disturbing about her parents, either in an artistic or a thought-provoking sense, they were straight up decent people, were always there for her.

The psychiatrist pushed her: Is there anything you may have forgotten, do you think, or repressed, from your childhood?

No, I don't think so, she says.

You think, but don't know?

What do we really know, she answered, lightly and not really asked as a question, more a statement.

The thing is – she says, almost didactically explaining her own strategy – that sex is the only thing that stops the massive discussion that goes on in my own head.

When you speak about 'the discussion in your head,' do you mean discussions that seem to be actual discussions, I mean voices that are discussing?

I don't know, she answers.

She becomes annoyed. The only point with the therapy, she thinks, is to eliminate all the unnecessary and random half-reasons for that which is troubling her and now they are sitting here and talking about her childhood for the nth time. As if a more or less "ordinary" life is not worth ruining. As if childhood is no more than a massive, elaborate deathtrap. She yawns on the way out.

After two weeks on the pills prescribed to her by the psychiatrist, her sight loses its focus. She feels different, without knowing what that difference consists of, or whether she has in fact always felt that way, the way many people feel, feel deep down inside that something is divergent from normality, even though it's not the case, the pills peel back the usual skin of melancholy, she is just tired, drowsy all day. There is something about her personality, she thinks, which was once nervous, deceitful, occasionally spiteful, but was one hundred percent her and she is now something different, somewhat more functional, but no longer recognisable: worst of all, she thinks, is that it does not bother her.

She has nowhere to go; she mainly stays inside. Obviously, she thinks, there are always places she could go, but there is no place where she is absolutely needed, or where someone will be waiting for her. She thinks that this creates a sense of freedom, but at the same time has a demoralising effect. It scratches at something in her which she can only describe as laziness. She receives sick pay and a monthly, although modest, amount from her parents. She always eats a banana and drinks a cup of coffee for breakfast. In fact this is the only routine she has. There is nothing else. All the vegetables in the fridge have developed a sort of moist fur on the outside. She thinks about putting them in the compost bin but keeps putting it off, it's as if she has lost interest. She used to see composting as a satisfying way to complete her own circle, her own natural cycle or something.

She flicks from one TV-channel to the next. Her favourite program is about pregnant sixteen year-old girls. They make her feel better. Better than them, better than many. She thinks: at least I'm not pregnant. But today she is just bored, gets annoyed by the girls and especially by those who become single mothers, how they make such a big deal out of it. Today there are no programs which manage to entertain her, but she still stares at the screen anyway, for hours, presses all the buttons, is a passive participant in a world of entertainment whose ideology turns out to be unsuccessful: not everyone allows themself to be anaesthetized.

Usually a piece of fruit and coffee. She takes an anti-anxiety pill followed by caffeine, which she acknowledges as stupid and certainly counterproductive, but at the same time it makes her feel less like an imbalanced person, trapped in a fragile body. She does a couple of yoga positions on the floor, before she gets bored and lights a cigarette on the balcony. Below her there is a ladder, it seems to be melted in place in the lower half of the wall façade, only has a few steps, she's never seen it used. From where she is standing and stretching, she can see a long way over the city, now just for the sake of the view, she thinks, it's a long time since she made use of it, the city that is, for anything other than finding a man to sleep with. It's rush-hour down there, she can see more people than she is capable of counting; without stopping her counting, from up there it looks as if they are stacked on top of one another, squeezed and mixed together. It is getting ever darker in the afternoons. She should clean the apartment, but being on the balcony, seeing and smelling, the odours have been clearer these last weeks, perhaps because the weather is sharper, cooler, and everything becomes more concentrated. From this angle, it's really quite impressive, she thinks, this is what you call a view. She sees how high up in the air she is, how far down the people down there are. How well do they know about it, down there? Probably not at all. One of the men down there must have known. He has moved between three points and at each point he stops and looks back to where he was standing before. He shades his eyes against the sharp light with his hand, looks up at her. She spreads out one hand in a wave without much conviction, testing, the man looks down the hill and walks on, along the street down there where she used to be. She has no reverse gear, she thinks. A kind of blindness. Does she give it enough thought? Yes and no.

She thinks about Espen, has been thinking about him since they ran into one another. How he acted in front of her then, was there not something different about him, something new, in his mannerisms and movements? She doesn't seem to remember that he was like that. Which sexual inclinations can lead them together again, she thinks, or was that just what separated them? And it is not that she wants him back, never actually wanted him, really wanted him, but there is still something there, is there not, or why is she thinking about him: maybe she just enjoyed how much he liked her, the confirmation of it. What was for him an important connection, a possible beginning of something with an obvious and unavoidable end station; a permanent situation which was their common future, was for her just a way of killing time. She liked the power it gave her, as the power sits with the one who likes or loves least. She liked that he didn't really know her and was therefore fascinated by her, that she could try to look different to how she felt. She'd have to tell the psychiatrist that he was right about that in their next session.

She is not an especially moral person. Nor a political one. She doesn't even vote at elections, not the one four years ago and not now. There is no pride in this, she doesn't think so. There must be something else which drives her. Self-absorption, perhaps. There is not much that really interests her. She is interested in relationships, maybe. But never the game-of-back-and-forth, where souls 'melt together' and where you love one another more than life itself, your own life, and on top of this are willing to give yourself up completely to this idea, for that's just what it is, she thinks, an idea, an imaginary edifice of the other person as you expect them to operate in compliment to your own self and all this violin-spaghetti-meatballs-construct, right up until you wake up one morning and catch sight of the long, black hairs which stick out of his nostrils and the box of tissues that is always on the bedside table begins to make you uncertain and repulsed, but maybe also aroused, what does she know, these men who all have the potential to be "the man in your life," but who eventually turn out to be interested in only one thing, and inattentive.

It's the physical that interests her, she concludes, the almost breathtaking physicality, to use and be used, to be fucked without a thought for what will happen after because it is unbearable. If you have done it right, you will not want to look each other in the eye afterwards, this is what she thinks.

74

It is not that she does not fall in love 'at first sight' and all that, it is more a question of having a 'realistic' view of how falling in love works and that she sometimes (though not always) almost manages to stop it, or at least tone it right down so as not to become hysterical and needy, a quality that makes her nauseous when she recognises it in others. Love is an inclination, she thinks, and so long as there is a little friction and no real harm done to either yourself or the object of your affection, then it is undoubtedly positive. It is good to be desired, but then it doesn't last especially long and everything becomes cold. One is distant, the other cries; finally everything descends into sarcasm. Then the dynamic changes, it's typical, she has realised, again this game-of-back-and-forth.

Seen through the eyes of her psychiatrist, the origin of this so-called "realistic view" of love is obvious. And various psychiatrists have been in agreement, several in this city, it's all so predictable it is impossible to not be in agreement about something so banal: she is afraid of rejection. And she pays for this, having to put up with it, she thinks and suddenly she becomes scared of her own anger, it has happened before that it has built up over a period, so that she becomes forced to lock the doors and grip onto a small stress ball in order to not lose her temper. This forced self-control, as the psychiatrist called it when she mentioned it to him, was just one more way of gagging herself. It was violent, she thought. It also scared her, just too much for her to have the strength to investigate it. She was good at that; distancing herself, as if placing thoughts and feelings outside of herself, thinking: this doesn't

75

concern me, he's talking about someone else. He doesn't beat about the bush, the psychiatrist, she can give him that, is at peace with it, and when at the end of a session he asked if she was having suicidal thoughts, she felt a kind of inadvertent pride over having qualified for conversations with him. She doesn't know what it's about and she can't help it.

In the tram on the way home from another therapy session she catches sight of Espen in the front carriage. Almost immediately, she recognises the blue, not particularly extraordinary jacket and instead of walking over to him as she otherwise normally would have done, without any deliberation, on the contrary, with self-confidence and conviction, she hurries out of the tram at the next stop, even though there are four more stops until where she actually needs to get off. Did he see me or didn't he? She doesn't actually believe he did. She runs towards the city centre. Her body is clunky, every step lands heavily on the sloping street, her feet sensitive against the cold asphalt, she's just wearing trainers. She doesn't get any real speed up, maybe because she is running down the longest street and the fact that she can see the end of it makes her painfully aware of her own shortcomings, she runs more and more slowly before she stops completely for a moment, grabs firmly hold of the back of a bench and stretches back and forth, casts a glance at an electronics store on the opposite side of the street, where the entrance is being fed by a queue that stretches all the way back down the pavement and disappears around the street corner.

And it's not that she hadn't understood earlier that there was something wrong, but it is as if this conflagration of the feeling she has and the action which follows it is brand new, a change from previously, she thinks, not just acting on

77

impulse but more like a connecting of cause and effect. And when she says that there is something wrong about it, she perhaps really means that there has been a kind of rupture with earlier behaviour and therefore an improvement? It's true that she is running away, that cannot be said to be unequivocally positive, but still: something new, different. She could go up to him, act flirtingly and half-vulgar, brought on both by her own desire and perhaps also the expectations she has convinced herself that he has of her. But she took herself away, removed her body from the consequences a meeting could bring about.

She finds a place to buy a coffee and reflect over it all. She leafs through the paper. A doctor is advising young people, especially men, to get checked out for STIs. As many as 70 percent of all those who get tested are women, a study shows. Outside the café there is an explosively colourful collection of bikes, all locked to the same stand. And beyond that, middle-aged men with downy heads on their way home from work, their pates reddened by a slowly setting September sun, their laptop bags knocking against each other on the way down the steps to the underground. On this afternoon, a completely ordinary Tuesday in September, a lack of shyness could have ruined the last week's breakthrough in therapy, just by smiling carefully at him, Espen, on the tram in rush-hour, she could have provoked the same self-destructive pattern which has defeated her so many times before. Back in the single bed, or any bed, or a piece of furniture, a heated floor, back to dominating and being dominated. She is not comfortable amongst men. She is only comfortable with men she is sleeping with. Although admittedly not completely, not even then.

The therapy room is humid. It is a small room with just one window, covered by pale, linen curtains. The effect of the light that slips in is somewhat apathetic although friendly in a way, maybe that is what they were hoping for, she doesn't know. On the wooden desk between her and the psychiatrist there is a box of tissues carefully positioned on her side, as if in suggestion.

When she recounts the assault that took place when she was fifteen, it is only because she feels that it is expected of her, in this room. And it's not because she has not told the psychiatrist about it, but the way in which she has done so, that has perhaps taken the gravity away from the actual seriousness of the act, if not for him, then for her. She says things like: I initiated it. She also says: I was not scared when it happened. She was loose and soft. She said nothing, for speaking would involve thinking. Being scared is first and foremost due to thinking, she says. These are the kinds of things she says in the therapy room.

The psychiatrist meets everything she says with a kind of stoical, clinical calm. Maybe she wishes for more friction, for him to react more strongly and be surprised, so that she can feel that he is taking her seriously and the seriousness can in this way spread to her. He says: I think you would take benefit from visiting the place where it happened, go to your school, to reconcile yourself with the act. But she carries the place with her, as it did not happen in his office, but to her body. This is not something she can rid herself of, even if she tries, even if she has tried.

Everything out here happens in slow motion, it's two o'clock in the afternoon, everyone is done with their lunchbreak but it's still too early to go home from work. It's quiet, just a few people are out on some errand or other, some pensioners, freelancers maybe. People with real weight. Around the corner is the publishing house where she worked for just a brief period, which she still thinks about with a kind of longing, as something she has thrown away and cannot get back. A couple of blocks further away, the paper. She won't go back there, either one place or the other. But if it brings out feelings in her which she can only think of as elegiac, it is probably because she finds herself in a transitory state, after something and before something else, after something old and before something new. If she wants, she can set something in motion. Holding back impacts the machine's rhythm, it just wants to move forwards. She walks into a shopping centre, finds the pharmacy. She collects her prescription, the chemist recognises her from previously, they nod to one another; the chemist knows that the pills are to be taken at the same time every day and that if they make her drowsy, she should take them before going to bed, she knows. The first time she was here, the chemist dutifully explained to her that there are two brands of the medicines, a cheap one and an expensive but that both had the same contents, the pills were identical: she could choose which brand she wanted, as if this is what she needed as she stood there collecting her first packet of antidepressants: a dilemma. She started to cry in frustration at the counter, not in an obvious way, making a scene, but more in a calm and clear "you are hurting me" fashion, which was enough that the pharmacist has since treated her carefully.

Everything she does is a masochistic act. That is not an exaggeration, she thinks. Almost everything she thinks about, how she doesn't like herself, for instance, that she is not a good person, stems from the same unrest, a sort of Deep Inner Conflict, to use the psychiatrist's words. Does she not deserve better? Both yes and no. When you take away all that is superficial, it's about being liked, loved even, or getting close to another person or to a kind of 'truth,' something like that. She takes no pleasure from it, other than the joy of things moving, of something being set in motion. But when it happens, when she is liked that is, she doesn't really feel much, that is to say she doubts whether it is in fact possible, unless this individual at least has certain illusions about how she is or how she thinks; in other words unless she has manipulated her way to affection from this other person. Maybe that's how the feeling is: painful. Horrible, repugnant.

From time to time she feels sorry for herself, like now, when she doesn't have anything, nothing at all which can frame her life and give her a sense of direction, as they say, or maybe the meaning to go along with the direction; no friends, even though just a couple of years ago she was constantly surrounded by close, vital girlfriends, whom she eventually pushed away from her by doubting how strong their connection really was and went to diverse and absurd lengths to reinforce the point, like sleeping with their boyfriends, that kind of thing. No unrelenting morals, no religion or idols.

There are some drooping, old flowers on the desk in the corner of the living room, the leaves turned towards the window, facing out to the yard. September will soon be over, apparent from the way the light fades earlier and the air has an almost clear and blue smell, but not as strong as when winter actually arrives, it is a way off yet. Over there, at the other end of the room, is an old fashioned hatstand, it came with the apartment when she moved in and who uses that sort of thing anymore, but as it's there she hangs her coat on it. The flooring feels cold and slippery under her feet. She looks out of the window and across to the neighbours on the other side, a red rug sticks out of a window like a tongue.

This is what will push her completely over the edge as regards love, commitment and so on, she realises, that she has begun to feel so alone and sad, that she is bored. That she misses Espen and that she has begun to admit, even if only to herself, that this is the case. Maybe most of all what she misses is being a part of something, doing something in a kind of community, it doesn't really matter with whom she thinks, now, not before.

It hurts. She needs something that can hold her together, a costume. It's certainly about time that she managed on her own. She is who she is, what else can she do but accept it, live with it. She keeps out what she has to. Everything

85

she is needs to be dug out now, she has to do most of the work herself. Occasionally she thinks about this as "staying alive." That it may look embarrassing, at least to some people whom she meets or speaks to, family or former friends, that she is choosing to stay alive. Why does she carry on, her specifically, for whom the future once seemed so bright but who has now let go of almost everything, closed herself off completely?

This is how she thinks now and then. Neither does she believe that there is a particular kind of mood which brings on this kind of question, it's more like a continuous debate in her brain, it's just there, neutral, in the way that a debate about one's own existence can be, but it does not generate any specific feelings in her. It's just something to be considered on a regular basis.

Espen calls. He wants to meet her, says that he wants them to talk. She says that she doesn't quite see the point. He replies that he doesn't understand what she means, as if the extent to which there is a 'point' isn't something to worry about, he just wants to meet, there doesn't need to be a 'point.' She hesitates. She doesn't like the way he is speaking to her, self-assuredly and if she thinks there is a point to discussing whether there is any point in meeting him, surely that is completely up to her to decide.

But she is dopamine's girl, cannot succeed, at least not for very long, in sparing herself the brief rush she gets from the attention, the interest he shows in her. They agree a time, she almost thinks that she is looking forward to it, to being seen, to being heard by him. There is not much that is either one thing or the other, she thinks, everything happens at once. Even if she is almost convinced that she doesn't want him, she still needs his attention, the will to meet her as she is. If she had not been so aware of these repeated swings in her emotions, and this with real help from the psychiatrist's eternal need to highlight both the one and the other, it would perhaps have surprised her, that she wants such divergent things at the same time.

Incredible that cigarettes have become so expensive, Espen says. I used to buy them for my mum when I was little, she sent me out with a small bag of money, they can't have cost much back then.

You're old, she says. And it's your fault, because you talk in a way that encourages people to think of you as, well, old. When you say 'back then,' it sounds like you're talking about at least fifty years ago.

Why is it that any time someone tells a story, it happened either five or fifty years ago? I've thought a lot about that.

You can't be older than thirty-six?

No. That's true. But if I talk about something that happened to my parents, it's always fifty years ago.

That can't be right.

He has started smoking, so she smokes with him. They are a little quiet to begin with, but the silence is sympathetic, respectful. There are no attempts at making smoke rings. It's almost too cold to sit outside the café, her muscles are taut, with her shoulders up by her ears; he is sitting completely still, calm, maybe he's not cold, at least not like her, or he doesn't show it. And even if she tries to make herself look nice, to be controlled, she doesn't manage, as her body is cold, almost clammy. She doesn't make herself putty, must instead be someone who braves the cold, become an animal then, tightens her shoulders, tenses, doesn't think about anything other than the discomfort, the cold and how it makes everything stiffen, her skin, lips, does she despise it? Or is there in fact a comfort in it, that in spite of everything she has needs which she recognises, which limit her, which she has to bow to.

He has to read about tennis, he says. Tennis is important, but only on TV and in the paper, he doesn't play himself. When he gets up in the morning, he starts by reading the most important news he can find about the sport, then he checks the weather and then conflicts around the world. It fascinates her, she cannot deny it, not the tennis that is, but the order in which he does this, because the fact that he is interested in tennis just annoys her, there is something about academics who are apparently obsessed with sport, she thinks, that mainly comes across as an alibi. To the right of where they are sitting cars drive by, close to them, she thinks about sitting in one of those cars, driving out into the country, the air pressure from oncoming trucks and lorries that make your own car tilt over so violently that you have to grip onto the steering wheel until your hands shake. She doesn't think Espen drives, it doesn't matter anyway, she doesn't ask.

What are you thinking about? he asks.

Cars.

I'm thinking about you, he says.

I didn't ask you, she says. He smirks at her. Now he's probably wondering what he's doing here, with her that is, when she gives so little.

And she is indifferent towards him, she can feel it herself. She's bored, wants to get something started, something other than empty words. Every now and then she contributes small witticisms and sends him long, attentive looks, but it isn't quite enough. They have the table between them and their hands neatly folded in their lap or under their face with their elbows on the edge of the table, eyes open towards one another, they breathe so lightly as to not be noticeable, their chests don't rise. Now that she is sitting across from him in this way anyway, she has a feeling of having lived in a parenthesis since they last saw one another and that all the small, unimportant things she has been doing in that time she has done alone seems to her as precisely that: unimportant. It is as if something is condensed in his company, she thinks, that she herself becomes realer in a way, or real full stop, even though he looks somewhat unmoved as he sits there smoking in front of her. He has a nice laugh, attractive hands. Maybe he can feel how she sees him differently now, fondly, warmly. She puts her overcoat on again, says that she is cold. He lights yet another cigarette, forms a cup with his hand around the lighter, breathes in deeply. He smokes while he blows the smoke out again, leans forward, looks at her face: Shall we go?

They stand at the bus stop, waiting without talking but just by looking ahead and back at each other they signal that they are going the same place. She shifts her weight from one foot to the other. They look at each other like two spies.

A bus arrives. It's tight, packed, every seated passenger is closed in by standing ones, staring into each other's armpits. They get onboard together and when they have each found a place, both standing in the aisle of the bus, right by the exit doors, he takes out a book. She doesn't want to ask him what he is reading, so she doesn't ask him what he is reading.

A brunette clutches a plastic bag of apples to her chest.

The bed is the same, as most of the things in his apartment are. Spartan in a way that only living alone allows, the necessities and little else. He hasn't decorated, not properly, as there is no point, assuming you believe that the alone state will cease in a foreseeable near-future. Espen has fallen asleep, she feels uneasy, sweaty and cold at the same time, as she sometimes can feel when she sleeps at someone else's apartment. It almost never happens at home, when she is sitting in her living room and reading or, more likely, watching TV, it's just here, with another and the physical spreading of warmth that she tries to not be afraid of. She lies on her stomach, naked and still too warm. He is one of those who sleep almost entirely motionlessly, his chest just about moves, the rest of his body is completely still. It makes her uneasy, how calm he is by her side, it creates more frustration and inner suffering than she manages to imagine. The whole right side of his body is touching hers, so it is impossible to run out now. She has to lie there, unmoving like him, stare at the ceiling and think that it is a syndrome she has, a lack of ability to decide what to focus on. It's not necessarily about her body, or about how he sees it and may like or not like what he sees, although throughout puberty she fought serious battles around her own body and weight, but about how she manages her own inner life, if he sees her in the way she wishes him to, not physically, but mentally, maybe, or intellectually, as some

92

would say, people other than herself. But consequently it is also about bodies, about sex, which for her has to do with this general self-image, with which she is so obsessed, how she carries herself and how she acts, which comes back to how she thinks: for her, this connection is clear.

Right now she could use a drink. If only to help her sleep. She rarely manages to maintain these self-inflicted mini-detoxes anyway. She used to drink a lot, it was the glue between her and others, made it possible to like them and for them to like her. She drank alone too, to keep everything else out. After a while she began, on the contrary, to feel clean and sober even if she had drunk, she didn't get drunk any longer, everything became clearer the more she drank, so then it lost its appeal.

It's hard to sleep. It always has been. Her passion for controlling her own time allows her to follow a different pattern, it doesn't matter when she sleeps, no one is waiting for her anywhere. It's not usually a problem, the fact that she does not sleep much at night, precisely because it doesn't have any consequences. Other than now, when she has to share in that which is Espen and an unalterable part of being him is sleeping at night, as most others do, those with work and responsibilities. You make most of life up, she thinks, routines and habits, or the lack of them, it creates a kind of entertainment, a template for life.

The reason she is thinking of this, how people make things up, is because she wants to make a distinction. That she makes things up herself and is aware of it, but does not make up that she is aware of it, it just happens. That when she makes things up, similarly to Espen and everyone else she has ever known, she is making up something different to them and they something different to her. Not just to see it, but at the same time to be aware that she sees it.

In the morning it is light. She's alone in the bedroom, it takes a moment before she realises where she is, as it's more than six months since she was last here, everything looks different in the daylight, a kind of sharpness, more striking. What's more difficult is to accept it; she falls almost immediately into an abyss of self-reproach and doubt, this is not where she should be waking up. She hears Espen rummaging about in the kitchen, she doesn't like the thought that he has woken up before her and so has seen her sleeping, relaxed, in his bed and in that way the edge has been taken off what is actually at stake, at least for her. Why is she incapable of defying her impulses? Is it down to some form of psychological idleness, or a defect? It's difficult to be sure, just as most things are difficult to be completely sure of.

He comes into the bedroom with a cup of coffee, she thinks that he must find a perverse pleasure in waiting on her. He strokes her hair and isn't that a bit creepy? This display of forced almost-love, they barely know each other, then he comes in with coffee. If only to be polite, what does she know, about his motivation, she doesn't need to know either, when she thinks about it, what if she just tries to enjoy this attention which she does need, this care, if nothing else. She doesn't need to think, as the thoughts are accompanied by fear, she remembers this thought process from before, is pleased with herself that she is thinking this way, it sounds sensible, zen-ish.

'Would you like some breakfast?'
'I don't normally eat in the morning,' she says.

He sits down on the bed, strokes her arm gently, they are quiet. Espen shifts and turns with his back, centres his body towards her. He tightens the watch around his wrist, fiddling, looks up at her again, keenly expectant. She forces out something she believes will be considered a smile, her chest throbs and beats. He asks if she is ok, perhaps feels how she is sitting as if petrified in front of him, as if inanimate. She does feel a kind of tenderness for him, a strong tenderness in fact, which tightens in her when she sees his open face in front of her. It's maybe above all a tenderness for the tenderness he shows her, and how transparent he is in it all, so open; he doesn't even try to hide his interest in her. And although she is very familiar with casual relationships, she still doesn't have a habit of developing even a touch of indefinable feelings for someone she has just slept with, at least for someone she has just spent the night with, as intimacy is not an evidence for her, but new, new and difficult in a way which awakens something, maybe a curiosity for something or other which in many ways lies out of sight, or has done, for a long time.

He takes her hand, warms it, because she is cold and uneasy, but open to an approach, he can probably tell. What if she just stays there, with him? Attached herself like a fridge magnet to the surfaces of his life. The psychiatrist has advised her several times to surround herself with other people to a greater extent and so far he hasn't exactly been wrong. Not exactly. But he has also advised against getting involved with the first person to come along, relationship problems can easily trigger a relapse and that is the last thing she needs. It's the sort of thing that AA members are advised to avoid, he says, which he knew that she knew was transferable to her own situation, given that her personality consists of up to ninety percent addiction to different things, perhaps five percent self-preservation instinct and the remaining five percent a kind of vague death wish. But say she stayed with Espen. She would try as hard as possible. Be nice, more authentic.

How does that look?

For example, like this:

Make breakfast for him in the morning, before he goes to work. Use the expensive utensils you find in his kitchen drawers, the ones that are never used. Even if he owns few objects or utensils generally, he is still lacking nothing, in case you wanted to stand in the kitchen and make a half-gourmet effort. Get to know it all, make the place and things your own. Make omelettes, grind coffee beans yourself. If you have the possibility to caramelise something, do it without hesitation. Stand ready behind the stool at the breakfast bar when he comes tumbling out of the bedroom and rubs his eyes, look at his smile and take it all in. When he disappears out the door, press your face to the glass of the window and watch him until the end of the street, where you will lose sight of him. You can see your breath on the glass. Draw something with your finger. You are not waiting for anything.

She lets him help her, because he doesn't understand that she needs it, or that he does himself. Between them, something non-committal. She thinks about the boundary you cross by giving yourself up, going under, sometimes she would say: Do what you want with me, but she is afraid of what that is, what he wants; when she stays silent, is it because she values his friendship, the insignificance of what exists between them?

Part Two

Four weeks ago he did something kind. To say what, like exactly what it was, would involve stripping the act of its worth and so would be at odds with its intention. Roughly speaking, he can say that it had something to do with shelter. Not that it should be understood as him having exactly given "shelter" to somebody, but neither would that be so far from the truth, if he had to say something on the subject.

Every morning when he leaves home to go to work, he counts. How long she has been there, not because it is easy to forget, but so that it doesn't take him by surprise. Over the last few days, he has felt a kind of angst at the idea that she may move in properly, but the angst itself also confuses him, given all he wanted, almost without interruption during six months of working together, was to have her, to be close her. And so he learns that it can happen: getting too close. He feels it all the way down in his stomach, that it is possible.

As he slides out of bed in the morning she grabs hold of his thigh and holds him back, says 'Don't go yet,' she is lying on her back, naked between the sheets, there is a faint smell of sweat, fusty and moist. She watches him while he gets dressed, trousers, shirt, socks and shoes. He leans over the bed and kisses her, asks her to stay. He doesn't know if he means it. When he goes out the door, she rolls over in the bed to her side, the one she has made hers – he has a double bed now – and faces the wall. He tries to be quiet, to not make too much noise with the keys as he lets himself out.

He walks alone to work and from a distance he can see the small white roses in the flowerbed on the right side of the street, next to the ethnic food shop that's about a kilometre from the office. It gives him a sense of calm, a feeling of continuity. 31 days now. Since she came and let her palms sweep across his kitchen worktop, he remembers it: how she touched the surfaces of his apartment; the kitchen table, the edge of the sofa, the chairs. As if she was inspecting it all, even though she had been here a couple of times before; maybe she hadn't seen, not properly.

There are magnets and post-it notes hanging on the suggestions board in the shared kitchen at the newspaper's office; reminders to clean up, throw away old food. Outside the sky is low and full of clouds. The grey clouds are wrinkled, undulating, wet. He opens a window. Energy drink cans are strewn over the worktop, he rinses them under the tap and puts them in a bag. The rustling noise of aluminium against plastic makes his ears itch.

He sits down to work. His desk is tidier than the others', it's just how he was raised. The PC, keyboard, a notepad, just one pen, a coffee cup and then a spare pair of glasses. He needs order, predictability. Technically, he is still a freelance journalist, but he always wears the temporary access pass so that it is visible on his chest, always tidies up the kitchen, picks things up here and there, in the hope of getting a permanent job. Chief critic is what he is aiming for, so that he can more simply live freely and productively in harmony with what he still sees as his primary concern, books, thoughts. His financial situation has meaningfully and negatively changed over the last month, since she moved in. Then there is the freedom which he misses, which he has taken for granted for years and not given a single serious or considerate thought before he lost it. And in step with the increased interest in Japanese literature both in Norway and generally in Scandinavia, and with his having read five or six novels about Japanese loneliness, he has felt an almost bestial need to be on his own, to get a feel for who he can be now, without and after her. It's an endlessly returning question and the need to be alone has grown beyond all reason.

He is unsure whether he is still respected by the other staff. They have of course got wind of his relationship with the so-called child prodigy, who they know has had a kind of breakdown and therefore has sought temporary refuge with him, so it seems. And that he has a degree and still doesn't seem to have any success, either in his private life or at work. Not to say that he does a bad job, on the contrary, but there are a good few, he can imagine, who think he exaggerates a little, takes his job more seriously than the role, or the lack of one really, requires. But that's how he does it, the job and how he does everything else: thoroughly, neatly and seriously.

What made her change her mind, he thinks, he's curious about the movement that must have taken place, because it is not obvious, not to him, he doesn't know if it is to her. And that he does not have access to it, to what it was that made her come back, on top of that to almost settle down with him, in his apartment, it happened so suddenly, he can't quite understand it. He thinks of her at home at his place now, maybe sitting by the window, which at this time is filled with golden light, a stripe cast over her lap and further across the living room floor, she sits there and waits for him to come home again, what else does her day consist of other than waiting there, for him? Does he represent something that he himself is not aware of, maybe, something that means he is irreplacable, something she needs or is lacking.

Erik comes over and suggests they have lunch together. Over orange juice, sandwiches and fruit he asks about the situation with Emilie.

I don't really know, he says. It didn't really end up as I'd imagined it.

No, says Erik and sighs kindly. Has she moved in now?

I don't quite know how it happened, but it does appear to have happened.

If anyone can understand, it's Erik, he thinks. Erik's repeated need for running from his family has never seemed to him particularly compassionate or worthy of praise but what is clear to him now and was not before, is that more than fleeing it's an attempt to find his way back to himself, to the version of Erik that no longer exists, that had to give way once both wife and child became part of everything, in all that which was once just his.

He receives a text message from her, it says 'Are you on your way home?' and he can't bring himself to answer it as he sits on the tram, three minutes away. There is not much about this situation, he thinks, which can be said to be normal or particularly giving, it's not love and it doesn't really look like anything special. So what is it? He doesn't feel especially tied to her, doesn't really know her well enough to feel that.

But he still likes her, that's not the problem. Some evenings he really values her being there, sharing something with him. On the weekends when they are sitting at a café, outside, he smokes a cigarette now and then and she steals the odd drag. Her hands which shake too much, even when she is just drinking juice. She always has bruises om her legs, blue, green, almost yellow, sometimes purple. He likes making dinner, eating together. They get by.

She sits in the living room, watches TV. She especially enjoys the so-called lifestyle programs, she laughs and points like a child at what's happening. This is definitely a side of her to which he was previously completely blind, although he had his suspicions about it, that she might be younger of mind than she initially made herself out to be. Sometimes he stands in the doorway and watches her hypnotised face before she notices him, the colours and movement on the screen that seems to flash across her white, creamy skin, her eyes open, wide.

He does not feel adequate as her boyfriend. He occasionally tries his best: indulges her, pays attention to her, caresses her. Sometimes he doesn't want to touch her at all. He shuts himself in the bedroom, there is a desk in there, says he has to finish some articles. Last week she asked: 'Are you hiding from me?', which he did not know how to answer, as it could not be more accurate and it was possibly visible too, in his face, it's difficult, impossible really, to know himself and so instead he mumbled something about there being a lot on at work and that he was still being given more responsibility, it's a lot, but he's enjoying it too, maybe he'll soon get a permanent position. Then she just turns over on the sofa, carries on staring into the screen until the images are caught on her face like small holograms.

One evening he orders pizza, vegetarian for her, one with salami for himself. They sit in front of the seven o'clock news and eat slices of pizza from their own places on the four seater sofa. That is, he eats while she picks at the crust of her own slice, nibbles at it then puts it back and has he actually ever seen her eat something, really eat something, chew and swallow? He can't recall having seen it.

I've rented my apartment out, she says.

You rented it out?

Yes, that's what I said. To a sweet, old lady, she answers and takes for the first time a proper bite of the slice of pizza, chews and swallows. Is that ok?

I can't see any reason why it shouldn't be.

Good, she says and then they are done with that, without him being quite done with it.

He sits at his desk and works again, without any rhythm, more by necessity, he squeezes out word after word at a slow pace, if he could only get some time alone, he thinks, he would have made space, space for her on his own terms. When it was convenient, he thinks, she could come over, have dinner and they could share a bottle of wine, talk about what had happened since last time, because it's those breaks he needs, time away from one another which only becomes meaningful when it is of a certain duration and they can then meet again and talk, talk with interest about what is happening, has happened.

In the evening, when they lie together in bed, she sticks her hand into his boxer shorts and gets a firm grasp on his cock, gets it to stiffen. Then she strokes it carefully, and it all happens while he is just lying there. He closes his eyes, lets her touch him, because he does want her to. Finally she has made him come, over half the duvet cover. As if she thinks that he will take a kind of narcissistic pleasure in lying in it, literally in his own wake. He gets up and takes the cover off the duvet, puts it in the laundry basket before he lies down again, under a naked duvet, she has turned away and is lying on her side, as usual with her body half visible, half naked towards him.

She has narrow feet, he notices, suddenly. They are long and narrow, he watches them while she leans forward over her own lap, paints her nails with red varnish. He has always liked the way she moves, because she's a slim girl and sort of hesitant in her movements, as if she is always thinking about something else, isn't completely present in her own wrapping. The living room smells strongly of solvents from the nail varnish, he thinks it is invasive, in the way he has started to consider her, like an invader, that is. That he is obliged to share most things, including himself, with her, at any given moment. Only at work is he free, as it is no longer possible to get anything done at home, it's as if she sucks everything into herself, even when they are each sitting on their own hard chair at the table and the distance between them, both physically and psychically, is so obvious for both of them that they can hardly look at one another, even then. Even then none of this belongs to him alone. He is divided and he wants out. There is no other way to say it, but he can never bring himself to say it. It's difficult, no doubt about it.

She tries to tidy up the nail varnish that here and there slips outside the edges, spreads out into the pores of the skin right next to the nail and hardens, dries and there is not much she can do about it. She sighs. Now and then she looks over in his direction, but just quickly, is probably aware of the somewhat indifferent face that meets her then and what is possibly going on behind it. Neither of them does anything. He can't imagine that she is not also aware of what has happened between them, he can't be the only one to feel it, this new distance that reigns over two who at one time shared something strangely pleasant, something obviously and undeniably good, at least a kind of tension. Then maybe he is waiting for her to articulate it, what it is that has changed, as cowardice is a characteristic he has nurtured since puberty. He thinks that it is easier to see the beginning of something than to see the end, or maybe it's the other way round. It's the beginning that inspires him, he has realised, which interests him in an almost literary fashion. Similarly to the anticipation which comes from opening a new novel and not yet being able to see the extent of what he is getting himself into. And the further into the book he goes, the more the story becomes limited – the possibilities that the writer opens with vanish – all the groundwork done at the start has consequences for the rest of the story, the possibilities are narrowed down, right until there are none left, just an ending.

CONTEMPLATING/COMPLAINING

One evening at the end of November, just after dinner, my boyfriend said that he wanted out of the relationship. He said it while we stood doing the dishes, me with the brush, him with the tea towel. The noise from outside the window, it was after all a Saturday evening, soft voices out there. The radiator hummed from the living room.

'Just now that we were starting to figure it out,' I said. Then I cried a little.

'I know,' he said. 'I know.'

He told me that my uncertainty had begun to wear on him, gave him a guilty conscious, how I projected it onto him: if he was in a bad mood, I decided it was due to something I had done and that he was about to leave me. In other words: the fear of being left led me to being left. That I tried to gain his attention the whole time, either by ignoring him, something he claimed to have learned to see through almost immediately, or by knocking the paper or phone or whatever else he was quietly sitting engrossed in, out of his hands, so that instead he could focus his full attention on me. He felt confused, he said, but undoubtedly discontented, possibly also spineless.

It was not that he wanted to break up with me – he spoke at length about how to begin with I had changed his life for the better, that I had helped to silence the doubts he had had to fight, about whether he was a person that it was easy to like, easy to talk to, easy to look at – but more that he felt it was necessary.

He was composed as always, careful and almost sympathetic, when he said that something was pulling him away, from us. I'd become paralysed, standing there, as if stuck to the kitchen sink, while he packed my things in a large backpack in the middle of the living room floor.

'It's as if everything you do and say is taken from an article in a magazine. Or a film. Or a book.'

The day after the breakup I bought a bouquet of flowers for myself. I wrote on the card: 'I am sorry that you will die alone.'

Not really, of course that didn't happen. But it was something I thought about, something I could have done. That is unfortunately the way my brain is screwed together. Completely by chance, it's screwed together like that.

Things couldn't get worse, they got worse. And what I felt, I couldn't quite put my finger on it, did he feel that too? Regardless of how needy and suffocating the experience of my closeness was for him, was it not painful to lose it all the same? It seemed probable. Why it was so important to me, knowing what he felt, I mean, and would come to feel, now that the cork had been pulled out between us, I could only ascribe to a kind of pride, maybe because I, although quite insecure, thought that it was quite simply humiliating that he should leave me and not the other way round. To anyone else, it must seem absurd, I thought. I was the one who was young, intelligent and attractive and, even if he was too, in his odd, creaking way, he was in equal measure socially awkward and stuttering, in a way that made him seem less intelligent than he was, or more intelligent in a way that no one was really interested in. But he did interest me and so must come to interest others. Sexually, mainly, to begin with, perhaps because he was the type of man that it was impossible to imagine having sex, in any case not in the same way that I did it. It definitely triggered something in me that I could not describe as mere curiosity, but also as arousal, the thought of seeing him in a sexual situation, seeing his face and expression, what his brain registered with me in front of him and how it articulated itself in his body just seconds later, in his cock.

He was intimate and intense when we slept together, in a way that was not familiar to me and even if I had long seen non-violent sex as passé and something you almost had to suffer through, it was different with him, because after a while I was able to appreciate his cool hands on my body, how it felt to really be caressed, touched, something like that. And with the rejection it became amplified, the sense of unassailability. With distance he became more handsome, more suitable, more of a loss, a large and painful one; I came to think that the relationship was like doing a jigsaw, where you sit with a piece in your hand and can't quite see the full picture or figure out where it fits in, with the rest that is, the whole and that if you could just flip the piece on its head or turn it in the right way, then it would fit, the way it is designed to do, the way we were and in theory could fit together, if only something was flipped or turned. That was where the hope lay and the hope was dangerous, I knew that: the hope would stop me moving on, would lock me into something which was really over, against my will, out of my supposed control.

It was not for nothing that this night was black as an olive, as I walked across the street, on the way to a hotel that was just a couple of kilometres from his apartment and the whole dramatic aftershock was nothing other than silence, that is to say not particularly dramatic at all. There was nothing else to do other than to hope that the separation would have the same effect on him, would benefit me. I had a kind of insight into these things as I knew that even if the decision was his and grounded in thoughts and considerations that I could not control, I could at least control how I reacted to it. Hence I shouldn't react at all, but instead respect what he saw as a correct and intelligent decision, it is probably for the best, as he said and then then the lack of an emotional reaction or protest from me would sow doubt about it all. I felt powerful, smart. As if the pendulum had suddenly swung over to my side, there was undoubtedly power, considerable power in having been left, in the way you have no particular responsibility. It is the one who has taken the step away who can end up harmed by the regret, a terrible and intense regret, without knowing if the harm is irreparable or not.

Back in my own apartment, the old lady who had taken over a while ago had now been moved into a nursing home. I'd imagined that it would look completely different, formed by her. But it was still there, the apartment, exactly like before, like a corpse. There were a few things that the old lady had left, that is to say: food, fruit and bread crusts, a couple of shrivelled vegetables in the bottom of the fridge. The living room smelled of something I can only describe as cloths, damp dishcloths used for washing up.

I took my Mac out of the backpack and opened my email account, there was a bill, a survey, a few adverts. But never a party, a launch, a vernissage, an invitation, like I often used to receive, when I was part of a mailing list connected to work. One problem with this city, I thought, was that people did not end up broken down or lonely at the same time as one another. So I would just have to wait. Waiting wasn't a problem, on the contrary, it was often a pleasure, sitting quietly and waiting for something to happen, without bringing it about personally and then suddenly it happens, the thing you've been waiting for, almost before you want it to. It made me feel that I was on my way somewhere, that something was in flux and thus valuable, and that keeping myself alive was essential, as something was coming, headed straight towards me. The world was quite a fascinating place when there was a mystery within reach. I stood in front of the mirror in the bathroom for almost half an hour, brushed my teeth with the toothbrush.

The next morning I woke early and went through the cardboard boxes I had in the storage room, full of newspapers and periodicals and magazines. I pulled out a sex magazine, if that is a name for anything, or is the name for everything. It was always there in the box in case I needed it, just like a pocket handkerchief in the right jacket.

Touching myself, as if to catapult my brain out of my head, had always proven to be particularly effective. I was wearing a t-shirt, skirt and ankle socks. I looked down at the t-shirt. It was from a swimming club in my hometown but if you just glanced at it, the logo could be confused with one of those t-shirts you buy in street markets in warmer climes, on holiday, because of the palms and sandy beaches that were pictured and which certainly had nothing whatsoever to do with swimming freestyle in an indoor pool. I undressed and put my clothes in a small mound on the floor before straddling the pile and starting to rub myself against it. I fetched a bottle of beer from the fridge and pushed it inside myself while I flicked back and forth through the magazine, looked at tits and pussies and cocks until I came. Then I fell asleep, immediately, and slept for almost two hours.

For a long time I let the more or less loving comedy that I had turned him into, in my own head that is, sort of stand in the way of the fact that he didn't love me, and that I felt it.

And why would he, I thought, when I had not invested much in him either, in emotional terms – there was something else I had taken with me into it, something that wasn't as pure as loving someone, which I after all had little experience with. Going in there, into his apartment, was disorientating. There is one kind of self-importance, I thought, the good kind, which makes you humble about your surroundings, other people, about your own limitations, nature and so on – but then there is the other kind: the poisonous, paralysing, offensive self-importance. The latter had shown itself to be especially relevant in this relationship. It didn't necessarily need to be because of him in particular, it could fundamentally be with anyone, the point is that the close relationship with another, being so intimately connected to someone, brought out this kind of self-importance in me and maybe in others, maybe even in him.

I knew that there was more than one way to demonstrate your love; through respect, attentiveness, those kinds of thing. But was that right? If you haven't been in other relationships, not experienced that the other person

122

unequivocally respected you, where he or she praised you for your goodness, your loyalty, your calm, how were you to get everything to look so simple? And still it seemed that it (respect, that is) really was more of a kind of admission, an admission that whatever he or she felt for you, it didn't even resemble love. This was the sort of thing that kept me awake at night.

There were a lot of colds. Women and men with harsh coughs in the underground. Everyone kept away from one another. Angry, suspicious eyes, fever dreams, swollen cheeks. No one bought anything from the Romanians who sold flowers along the main road. In the quiet, dark morning hours there was no one who spoke, as if it wasn't morning at all but late at night.

I thought a lot about how I hadn't cried much since it happened. It didn't resemble grief, more a kind of disconnection. Every morning I got up in the old, bleak apartment, made coffee and ate breakfast, to then read for a couple of hours on the sofa, which faced towards the windows. Later I went out and looked around, wandered aimlessly about town while I took in the day's atmosphere and smells, people on their way here and there. It gave a definite calm, now and then I felt that I was capable of living without the imagined symbiosis that was he and I, like it was before, even if I wouldn't have managed that either, it was more about keeping going; other times I realised that I had hardly lived a life at all. The only pride I had left was in not contacting him, that I had at no point done anything as insignificant and noncommittal as sending him a brief text message, I was too stubborn for that. It never crossed my mind to reach out a hand to someone who had lost interest in me. I considered it genuinely, emotionally healthy to distance myself in this way. Then I could make a decision as well – decide to not protest or to react emotionally to his decision. That was the only weapon I had.

I filled the apartment with green plants, like I had seen other people do on the internet. I looked for jobs and studies, something that could give me a sense of direction. There were no men, other than the ones coughing in the underground and who in any case did not generate any form of lust in me. They weren't unlike the plants I had in the living room. Stand there, present in the world. It doesn't make any difference for someone who has started again.

I read the news, kept up with burgeoning conflicts, I had actually become quite good at predicting them –it's now just a question of time before it all really explodes into something horrible in, for example, Sri Lanka – stuff like that, I could see it all.

The nights I actually slept, I had chaotic dreams. They were often about previous relationships, romantic or otherwise, but where in every instance I was rejected or hurt, abandoned. In an especially brutal dream, one which kept returning, I opened a door to a room and found Espen there in bed with someone else and when he caught sight of me in the doorway he didn't react, I mean not at all, just looked at me, didn't care, carried on with the girl who in the dream had neither a face or a name. How typical was that, I thought, how the other woman in the dreams had neither face, name or personality. Like a doll. Like those new, lifelike sex dolls you can buy on the internet.

Occasionally my ex visited me, the one before Espen, we slept together, he was moody and not very attentive, I slept next to him and put my arms around him while he breathed beside me. That's how it was with intimacy. That's how it was with anything.

He came and went for a few weeks, we had sex as much as several times a day, with restrained feeling and with help from various battery-powered items that made the whole thing possible. You could say, it wouldn't be inaccurate to suggest, that there was something deeply tragic about it all, two people who had once been close and now were not so at all, just in this amputated sort of-fashion, out of a lack of anything else.

At the start of November I got a job. As a kind of hostess at an art gallery. The visitors to the gallery consisted mainly of tourists, all in waterproof anoraks and walking shoes. Most of them weren't there to see art at all, but to ask me if they could use the toilets or which way it was to a larger gallery at the other end of the city centre. I dutifully gave them directions to the other gallery but never let them use the toilets. If they were in a hurry they could always squat on the floor, leave it there and call it art. I enjoyed it there, just five hours a day behind the desk in the corner of the room, the gallery, where the exhibition changed every third month and my only responsibility was to make sure nothing was stolen, that the lights were turned off in the evening and the doors locked properly. It suited me perfectly. If it hadn't been for the off seasons I could have worked there for the rest of my life, like a small Russian doll in a larger Russian doll, without being held responsible or being in danger of ruining anything, doing any serious damage.

It was altogether relaxing, sitting in there, surrounded by art and just a couple of curious people every hour, well paid too and when the light faded in the evenings and I was once more alone with the paintings, I felt a calm which was limited to these few, short moments and which would not occur again until the next day, the next evening in the gallery. Only here was it all ok. It was fine to be born here, or to come here to die. I wasn't doing either, just existing in between and that worked fine, too.

One evening, almost exactly two months after it was over, a letter arrived. I didn't open it when it came, as there was no doubt as to who the sender was, it had to be Espen as no one else wrote letters, no one else I knew wrote letters and I didn't know that many people anyway. Instead I decided to wait until the next day, to open it at the gallery after I had turned on the video installations and the lights and the calm had descended in there, that would be right for a letter, I thought. So I opened a bottle of red wine, sat there in the sofa and stared at the letter, drank and tried to distance myself from that which, unannounced, had glided in under my door and was there not in any case something tiresome about sending letters, something that said read me, read me, read me and moreover: answer. That is not something you can expect of a person.

The next day I read the letter as soon as I got to work. It was particularly quiet at the gallery that day, the air was stuffy and almost claustrophobic, a warm day, unusual for this time of year. He wrote that he wanted to meet, as it had not felt right since the time he threw me out and when on top of this I had not answered the letter where he shamelessly admitted all his worries and feelings, those feelings had only been amplified. We could get a coffee, or a beer, if I didn't want to have dinner, because that was an option too, he wrote, he would pay. Just call me, he wrote and it came across as actually quite pitiful, I thought, he did too no doubt; perhaps he didn't have that much to lose.

And myself, what did I have to lose? In the period from when I moved home and up until the letter, and thereby he, showed up again, what had there been, other than a sort of vague grief? Lots else, obviously. The everyday, obviously. Lunches and coffees and walks and work, but was that not the same as everything else, that is to say: most things, in a way, had faded somewhat? Had it not been grey at night? And had I not some nights heard myself talk about him, talk about him so much that even I got bored of hearing about it? Yes, of course. Of course it had also been like that. But how much was it about him, really about him and what he left behind in me, or just about me, just the inner conflicts with which I was still tussling, I

130

couldn't say, not with certainty. If I had to think about it, what the cause of the doubt or the loss was, how would that be useful, how could I ever feel at home where I was, back in the old apartment, if every doubt had to be examined, resolved? It did not help to think too much, especially not about that which didn't really have a logical conclusion but which was driven by feelings and thereby a whole heap of other variables, like mood, energy levels, supposed "match fitness," things like that. It didn't help.

I called him the same evening. The conversation was short and not particularly emotionally charged but there was undoubtedly expectation there, possibly also longing.

I'm glad you called, he said, cautiously testing, almost fragile.

Yes?

I thought maybe we could meet and talk. Are you free tomorrow?

Where?

At one of our apartments, maybe? That was where the expectation lay, and the possible danger, I thought.

I think it's best if we meet out somewhere.

If you prefer. I know a place.

So it was agreed, we would meet. It was something concrete and concrete is always easier to relate to than vague, blurred. It was simplicity that I wanted.

That evening I got ready as usual, washed my face with cleanser, showered and went to bed. I didn't know if there was anything else to understand, if the meeting would bring some kind of clarity, or if clarity was even something to aspire to. Was it not irreparable, I thought, that which had been and now was no more? There were no clear feelings, no real insight into what it was that had taken place between us, either in the beginning or during or in

132

the end. Maybe a kind of power play, a distance which we had both tried to dissolve. To escape something in ourselves, was it possible to think that way?

There was a wooden fence which closed in the terrace, but the bird table with a roof was the first thing I noticed, the wooden arms which held up the suet balls in different sizes, surrounded by small birds and pigeons fighting for space; it was a strange sight, this fencing in of almost-nature in the middle of the city. It was Erik who had introduced him to the space he said, and there was nothing surprising about that specifically, I thought, at the same time I allowed myself to be surprised.

On the way here I had thought a lot, about how I, in one or various ways, was a prisoner in the monotonous melodrama that the loss of him had unleashed and that this was why I had accepted to meet him, because I couldn't see an obvious and definitive way out of it. And even if he was never great company – a dog would have been better, as towards the end of the relationship he neither said anything much or touched me, just when it was absolutely necessary – I still felt a strong need to sit across from him, here, at a café that at best was kind of cute, but strange, really odd and which in a way magnified the unsaid or that which was the obvious abyss between us. He was nice, I thought, nice and decent and pretty smart too, not a genius, but in a way that you could approach, recognise yourself in, feel a connection with. But garrulous he was not, that was not something that could be said about him.

He took hold of my wrist and squeezed cautiously. I've missed you, he said.

You shouldn't have thrown me out, I said and pulled my hand back.

It was a long time ago. There are other things we can talk about.

Like what then?

Are you well?

Everything is fine. Really fine, all of it, I answered, as if rephrasing it made it truer.

His face was thin and dry, like someone who – without knowing it – had once been very handsome but who now only resembled disappointment. There was no other way to explain it. My own face, I felt, was a way of speaking. A metaphor, perhaps, but for what I didn't know, perhaps for what was happening on the inside, what had happened since the last time.

The day he ended it, while we stood doing the washing up in the kitchen, I had felt a kind of vague feeling of lightness, I came to remember. Where did the lightness come from? That I had gone round and feared it for so long, that he would break up with me, and as the fear of something is almost the same as waiting for it to happen, the lightness. Just that.

He moved closer to me, suddenly looked simple, but good, without the sunglasses which he had put down on the wooden table. He leaned forward and kissed me on the forehead.

You love a person who doesn't love you? How common is that? I said and stared at him, at the space between his eyebrows.

But that's not how it works, he said merely, briefly and after a long pause.

But who cares, I thought. Do I care? Only a little. Just enough to ruin every day.

I smiled at him and wondered how I looked.

Also by Nordisk Books

Havoc
Tom Kristensen

*You can't betray your best friend
and learn to sing at the same time*
Kim Hiorthøy

Love/War
Ebba Witt-Brattström

Zero
Gine Cornelia Pedersen

Termin
Henrik Nor-Hansen

Transfer Window
Maria Gerhardt

Inlands
Elin Willows

Restless
Kenneth Moe

We'll Call You
Jacob Sundberg